Wilcox PFC:
~ Rayzor Zombie War Series Book 3 ~

by Richard Howes

Wilcox PFC: Rayzor Zombie War Series Book 3
By Richard Howes
All rights reserved
Copyright © 2018 by Richard Howes

Excerpts held by Richard Howes

Published by: LRCK Publishing

Publication date: 07-01-2018

ISBN-13: 978-0-9849969-5-7
ISBN-10: 0-9849969-5-8

Cover Art by LRCK Publishing

Introduction:
I liked and hated John Wilcox when I first created him. As the writer of the Rayzor Zombie War Series, I can do that. Can't I? As you know, he was a redneck, chewing tobacco spitting, jerk to Julie Rayzor, and then he shows how much of a hero he is in Book 2: RayzorWire. Why? I asked myself that a thousand times. Then I decided to explore his motivations. This is his story.

To my Rayzor Zombie War Series fan: Thank you!

This work is a prequel to Books 1 and 2. I debated labeling it as a prequel in the title, but I expect I'll have a couple more of these and thought that sequential numbering would make it easier for you. This is "Book 3." It's also written in 3rd person so you can see and enjoy the different aspects of John Wilcox's story from different perspectives. Please don't hate me for any of that!

I apologize for my delays in writing another "Julie" novel. I've kicked around ideas for a tale that's "15 years into the future," another "Army mission," or "Julie goes back to the Ozarks with her friends." Let me know what you would like to see.

I deleted long apologies for the delay. I have no real defense. (Well, I could have excuses, but excuses never matter!)

Chapter 1 Hunter

John Wilcox steadied the rifle, peered through the scope, and aligned the cross-hairs on a deer. Adjusting his aim, he drew an imaginary 'X' from opposing ears to eyes. He exhaled, paused, held his breath, and squeezed the trigger. The .308 frangible round turned brains to mush and dropped the doe.

He breathed again, harder and faster with the excitement of the kill. Another fifty pounds of venison provided food for his mom and siblings.

Leaves crunched.

John drew his handgun and turned. Mountain lions roamed the Arkansas hills in violation of State Department of Agriculture directives and subsequent denials. He'd seen tracks as big as a man's hand.

"Hidey Johnny!" A red-haired, preteen boy appeared through the trees. "Grrreat shot." Danny drew out the 'r' in a heavy Ozark accent.

"Danny, help me gut it. Then we'll butcher it in the shed. We gotta get the venison into the smokehouse. Y'all need to finish the work. I won't be here to do it." He pushed his handgun back into the holster.

John realized Danny had watched the hunt in complete silence. That skill took practice and dedication to perfect for any noise alerted and alarmed deer, sending them leaping away. John started teaching his brother when the boy was six years old–taking down squirrels and rabbits with a scoped .22 rifle. The boy had been hunting for four years and might be able to gather food through the fall while he was away if Samantha helped him with the carcasses.

"Mom said lunch would be ready in about an hour."

"Lunch? A long way for y'all to walk to tell me." After resting the rifle against a tree, John opened a can of Skoal and positioned a wad of chewing tobacco into his cheek.

"I didn't have anything to do. Mom said she's making a big dinner tonight before ya leave tomorrow."

John smiled but didn't respond.

"Y'all've been gone since before sun-up. Y'eaten at all?" Danny scratched his ear.

"I wasn't hungry until you said something. Now I'm starved." John pocketed the tin and shouldered his rifle. He pointed to the ATV. "There's some jerky in the backpack on the four-wheeler. Take it down to the deer, and I'll meet you there."

He turned to hike the eighty yards to the clearing where the doe fell but stopped when he didn't hear the ATV engine start. He looked back to see Danny had unstrapped the pack from the Honda and began to drag it through the brush.

"No. Danny," he called up the rise. "Drive the quad."

"All right!" Danny smiled as he turned back and hefted the pack onto the vehicle.

***

Within thirty minutes they'd chewed up the jerky, hung the deer from a tree, cut the arteries to drain the blood, gutted the carcass, stuffed it with freezer packs from the cooler on the quad, and strapped it to the front rack. Danny rode behind John as they followed the trails home–a two-story clapboard farmhouse.

He parked by the shed and hung the deer on a skinning rack.

"You are so much stronger now." Danny shuffled his feet.

John nodded without comment as he retrieved a fine-grade sharpening stone from the tool crib inside the shed.

He raised his knife and spat on the blade. Working it in long smooth strokes, he honed the edge to razor sharp.

"The army made you buff. Months in boot camp." Danny watched and learned from his older brother.

"The food is good too." John realized how poor the family was. How sparse the food table had been for himself and his mom, little sisters, and middle brother. His teenage cousin, Beauregard, moved in two years ago when the boy's parents died in a car wreck–them drunk-driving.

"Hey, Johnny. Do you remember Dad?"

"Yeah."

"I wish I did."

"You were a baby."

"How old were you?"

John thought for a moment and said, "I was ten. Same as you are now."

"What was he like?"

"Brave. Died during the war, saving a bunch of guys, and killing terrorists. Nominated for a Medal of Honor."

"What's that?"

"The highest award a soldier can get."

"What's nominated mean?"

"It means the government is thinking about giving it to him."

"I'd give it to him."

John recalled his mom's two jobs. Working at a bakery from the early morning hours until noon and then waiting tables at a diner until long after dark. She'd worked them forever. A military honor doesn't pay in cash. "I'd give it to him too, but it doesn't buy groceries."

Danny asked, "Are we poor?"

"We make do." John frowned as he recalled the donated food and church-goer's hand-me-downs he had helped his mother collect since he was a child. Everyone had a kind word, but he had heard the whispers that he didn't fully understand until recently.

"Then we're poor?"

John nodded. "It's getting better."

"Who was that other guy?"

John asked, "What's-his-name?"

"Yeah." Danny laughed.

"That guy fathered Janine and walked out... Six years ago."

"So he's Janine's dad?"

"Sperm donor."

Danny's face scrunched up. "What's that?"

"Ask me again in five years." John's thoughts plowed on. They wouldn't suffer anymore. The army paid twice what the factory gives a teenager if he didn't buy anything and ate only in the mess hall. Mom cashed the checks, but I'm only four months in, taking Army Corp of Engineering and demolitions training. The bigger paychecks will come with corporal, but that'll be a couple of years.

He'd joined the army, he thought, because it offered a life he respected, but upon realization, it provided security. He appreciated the military because his father, James Wilcox, and his paternal grandfather, Robert, were soldiers. James got called up to active duty from Reserves fourteen or fifteen years ago. The man returned home twice a year for holidays and between rotations out-of-country. He died just after Danny was born. John recalled that Danny was ten. Sammy was two years older than Danny.

John remembered everything his father had taught him about hunting over those early years. They'd harvested squirrels, rabbits, and deer. They fished the river. He recalled every moment when his father was home, and he learned most of what he knew about living off the land from the man. Somehow, they both knew the skills would help, and they did after his dad died and the life insurance and government death-benefit money ran out.

His mom, Kimberly, had dated a professional-computer type guy. Peter. That's his name. Peter Ponca. The man was angry when John wouldn't take his last name. Why would he? He wasn't Peter's son. That relationship lasted just a couple of years. They'd moved into a three-bedroom condo, but Peter bailed six months after the wedding. Kimberly discovered that the man hadn't done paying-work in years and was living off his inheritance until the money ran out, and he wanted Kimberly to take another job. She'd just accepted a third job when she found out she was pregnant with Janine, and the Peter Ponca left. He'd seen Kimberly's belly getting bigger and knew it wasn't belly-fat. John knew Peter didn't want to stay home and take care of an infant, as well as John, Sammy, Janine, and Danny.

John was twelve years old then, and he'd babysat, fed peanut-butter sandwiches or hotdogs, cleaned spills, and settled fights over the TV channels while his mom worked, and Peter went to the bar, coming home drunk, happy, never abusive or bitter, but refusing to work or spend time with kids.

Kimberly moved the family to the old farmhouse. John lost his friends and found work. His school years were spent mopping floors and hauling flour sacks at the bakery, working beside his mom, before class-time, then going to the town library after football and basketball practice, and weekend shifts at the packaging plant. He often missed practices to work. Kimberly made sure he went to his game nights. The money was more important than going to all the practices and workouts, but he believed that maintaining a commitment to teammates and family was more significant than everything. That faith harmed him when He'd fallen behind in school and then again when he'd joined the Army. His old buddies abandoned him, and they probably felt the same for they went to truck driving school, road crews, factory work, or the gulf coast to work fishing boats. The old team was gone with the wind and the tides. He had new buddies in the Army and he had his sibilings and mother. Through all his losses, he never forgot that his childhood meant being a big brother and, in some ways, a father-figure to his siblings.

"You got a lot of deer." Danny interrupted his thoughts.

"Only had two weeks off. Wish I got more." John sliced at the hide on the deer, cutting it expertly. "I want to tan the skins. Would make good work-gloves and maybe a vest or jacket. I won't have time now."

"I'll do it." Danny smiled.

John saw that Danny might hope to impress him. He already was.

"Do it, but be careful. There are some nasty infections you can get working with this stuff." He looked at his own hands and realized he wasn't wearing gloves. "Gloves will keep you from cutting yourself. You don't want to get any of this in your skin. It'll make a bad infection."

"How bad?"

"Could lose your fingers or a hand."

Danny's face scrunched up at the idea.

"I wish I taught you more about hunting."

"I can hunt." The boy's face turned red as he clenched his fists.

"I know, but there's more. Stuff dad taught me that I could teach you and Sammy." He'd tried to teach Samantha, Danny's older sister by two years, but she didn't take to the outdoor life. Not like Danny did.

"I read all the American Hunter, and Field And Stream

magazines at the store."

"When do you do that?" John used the knife to separate cuts of meat from the deer.

"After school, the third week of each month when the new issues come in."

"I used to do the same thing." John surveyed his pencil-thin brother, standing skinny as the rest of the clan, with an exception for Beau, their obese cousin. The kids lacked food despite John's Army paycheck going into the family account each month.

"Four deer will last." Danny stacked the steaks and went into the shed to retrieve a roll of butcher paper and tape.

"We don't need that. Gotta age it first. The weather is still too warm to cure it in the shed. We'll have to put it in the fridge. Check it every day and make certain the little fan I put in there is still running. One week in the fridge, then to the smokehouse, then to the freezer."

Danny nodded and returned the supplies.

John asked, "Mom's buying enough food?"

One of Danny's shoulders rose.

"Does she keep the fridge full?"

Danny shrugged again. "I guess, but Beau is always stuffing his fat face."

"Why won't mom make him get a job?"

"He got a job at the convenience store but got fired after a week. Bobby said he was eating everything." Danny laughed.

"Was that before or after he got fired from the warehouse?"

Danny's shoulders rose again.

John said. "You need to eat more and lift weights."

"I play soccer and basketball. Might try out for football next year."

"Football is good."

"When are you coming home again?"

"I don't know. Might get a few days away at Christmas. Army school ends then, but everyone's talking about deployment. Devon and Paver say Iran. Sarge said North Korea."

Danny shook his head at the far-away places. "Don't get killed."

"Break a leg."

"What?"

"Don't tell someone not to get killed. You say, 'break a leg.'"

"Why do you want to break a leg?"

"It's bad luck to wish someone good luck."

"I don't get it." Danny's face wrinkled up.

"It's like this... Instead of saying, 'Don't get killed,' you can say, 'Good hunting.' That way, you wish bad luck on the enemy."

"And that's okay?" Danny thought for a moment. His brow and lips pressed. "I hope the enemy breaks a leg."

John laughed. "Close enough…" He retrieved a mason jar filled with salt and mixed spices from a shelf in the shed.

Chapter 2 Cousin Beau

The screen door on the back porch clattered. Beau tromped down the steps and walked over. "Got another one, Little Brother?" he asked.

John hated the term and ignored his cousin. Beau was a year younger at seventeen, same height, same familial red hair, and eighty pounds heavier. He eyed his cousin's obesity.

'Dog,' the family's mixed-breed brindle-colored razorback sauntered around the shed to sniff at the deer on the table. John petted it and promised it a bone.

"I told Johnny I'm playing soccer," Danny said.

"Soccer is for towel heads," Beau said as he took a beer from the shed refrigerator and popped the top.

"Get me one of my beers," John said, indicating he'd bought and paid for them.

Beau looked at John with flat, dull eyes that flicked to the beer in his hands and back. The boy didn't move.

"Don't you have a job to go to?" John asked, his tone rising, carrying annoyance. He watched Beau drink his beer as he rubbed handfuls of the spices into the cuts of meat.

Beau swallowed and said, "I got laid off."

"You got fired."

"No. It wasn't like that. The price of oil dropped, and they laid everyone off."

"You didn't work in the oil industry," John said.

"Doesn't matter. We sold steel to everyone." Beau unclipped a folding knife from a belt loop and picked up a stick. He whittled away at the wood.

"Then why did they let you go?" John spat a stream of chewing tobacco on the ground.

Beau didn't answer.

"Y'unt blow some stuff up later?" Danny took a handful of spice and helped John season the meat, inexpertly slapping it.

"Maybe." John glanced at Danny.

"Come on?" The boy's eyes widened.

"Do we have anymore Tannerite?"

"Yeah!" Danny brushed his hands on his pants and grabbed a plastic jar off a shelf in the back of the shed. He shook the powder.

Beau said, "That will be fun."

Danny put the container down and returned to John's side.

John handed the boy a cigarette lighter. "Why don't you get the coals started? We need to get that other deer smoked and make room for this one in the fridge. You know where the charcoal is?"

Danny ran to the smokehouse and opened the wood stove. He went inside the shed and dragged out a bag of charcoal and then retrieved a sack of hickory wood chips.

"Are you still sick?" John kept his eyes on his work, not looking at Beau.

"No. I'm fine. I had a bad go. But I feel great now." He folded the knife and clipped it to his belt loop again.

"We're almost done," said John as he opened the fridge, took a beer for himself, set it on the table, and then pulled out four plastic bins of meat soaking in water. He lifted the containers onto the table top.

John popped the beer, downed it in one pull, tossed the can in a trash bucket, stacked the fresh cuts of meat onto the refrigerator racks, and checked the tiny electric fan set on a shelf inside the fridge. He turned back to the table and pulled the cuts of cured meat out of the water and scrubbed away the salt-rub 'skin' with a scouring brush.

"They soaked all morning," John said.

Beau watched with brain-dead eyes.

John glanced up and scoffed.

The rancid water went into the grass and gravel driveway, and the scrubbed meat went back into the empty bins.

John stacked two containers and jammed them into Beau's hands. Beau staggered under the weight, and he nearly dropped them.

"This way." John picked up the other two bins and walked to the smokehouse.

Danny poured lighter fluid over charcoal, stuffed crumpled newspaper inside, and lit the stove. The lighter fluid ignited.

"We should have started the coals earlier," John said.

"I did wha' ya…" The boy grew timid as if he'd done something wrong.

"Danny. I'm not mad at you. I should have started the coals earlier. We have time so that we won't worry." John turned to look at Beau but found he'd stayed behind.

Beau had returned the bins to the table and poked out the eye of the deer with his sharpened stick. A stupid smile crossed his face.

"Hey," John yelled. "Bring those bins and get me another beer."

"Okay," Beau said, but he didn't comply.

"And don't drink one yourself," Danny hollered.

Beau churned the eye-socket, stirring the fluid, and lifting it, watching the mess drip from the end of the stick. When Beau heard Danny, he stopped and looked up, staring at them across the lawn.

"Beau's milk-toast," Danny said.

"Where'd you hear that?" John asked.

"You said it."

John raised his voice. "I need that… Aw, fuck it." John headed back to the shed.

Kimberly Wilcox appeared on the porch. "Lunch, guys."

"Okay, Mom." He waved. "We'll be done in a minute."

John's phone rang. He checked the name, hoping that his guys hadn't changed plans for getting to the fort. The phone displayed Ellie Keating's name.

He answered her call. "Hi, Bay-bay."

Ellie laughed. "I love it when you call me that!"

John smiled, "You are my baby."

"You're leaving soon."

"Tomorrow morning."

"Do I get to see you tonight?"

"Mom's making dinner. Do you want to come?"

Ellie was silent.

"No?"

"My grandma is at my parent's house, and I only get to see her a couple of times a year."

"You go do that. Maybe we can go out late."

"Can you pick me up around nine?"

"You got it."

***

That evening, after a feast of a dinner, John pushed his chair back. "Mom, you spent too much."

"You haven't had dessert yet so shush-up and enjoy." Kimberly took the dishes to the sink. As Danny and Samantha rose to help her, she said, "Not tonight. Go play a game in the living room."

John said, "It's just that..." He wanted to mention Beau but stopped himself. "We have eaten so much. I'm worried there's not enough..."

Kimberly walked around the table and leaned to kiss him on the top of the head and wrap her arms around him. "You don't worry about food. There's enough food in this house, and there always will be. I'll bring out pie and ice cream. Go play a game. They love spending time with you."

He rose and returned her hug.

"Janine," John said. "You pick the first game."

"Chutes and Ladders." Janine hopped up and down and waved her arms, then ran to the game closet.

Groans rose from Danny and Samantha as the family moved into the living room.

"Just two games and then Danny gets to decide."

Danny grabbed a deck of cards off an end-table.

"Crazy eights."

"After Chutes and Ladders." Wilcox pulled the armchair closer to the coffee table and sat.

Janine pushed the game box on the table and threw off the lid. Samantha helped her set up the board and pieces.

Beau skulked by, heading up the stairs to his room.

Kimberly leaned her head into the hall from the kitchen, "Beau. Play a game with the kids."

"I don't feel well."

"Milk-toast can't hold his liquor." Danny riffled the deck of cards.

"Shut up, Danny" Beau said as he climbed the stairs.

John clenched his fists.

Beau, leaning down to glare at the boy from half-way up the steps, glanced at John. He mumbled something and disappeared.

Kimberly brought two bowls of ice cream at a time into the living room and passed them out, making two trips even though John offered to help.

"Mom?" Danny asked.

"Yes?" Kimberly asked as she handed him his bowl.

"What's a sperm donor?"

Kimberly's eyebrows rose as she looked at John.

He frowned.

She laughed. "Ask me when you are eighteen."

"Why won't anyone tell me?"

***

Two hours later, Kimberly sent the kids upstairs to take baths and check for ticks–girls first.

"Aw," Danny complained and threw his hands in the air and down again. "The girls take too long."

"Then you go first," she said as she helped Johnny pack up the board games.

"Aw," the girls said in unison, giggling at Danny, and

imitating his flapping arms.

"Girls. You go second. Now get upstairs. I want some quiet time with John."

The younger siblings trod the steps, and John went with his mother to sit at the kitchen table.

"Mom. It's about Beau."

"Don't worry about him." Kimberly brought two cups of tea to the table. She plopped them down, and the tabs and strings clung to the sides, wet from sloshing.

John spooned sugar into his cup. "He doesn't work. He got fired from the factory job. He disappears every night, and God knows where he goes to–Just walks down the road. I've seen him with his thumb out. He doesn't get home until after sun-up, and then he sleeps most of the day."

Kimberly put a hand on his hand. "Don't worry about Beau."

"I do worry. He's a bum. Beau drinks beer 'bout all the time. He's eating us out of house-and-home."

"You know his mom and dad died in a car accident. Claire was my sister. He's family."

"He can go to California. He's got an uncle there." Johnny scooped the tea bag from his cup and squeezed it with his thumb.

"Beau's uncle had six kids of their own... And you know, dear, Beau's not that bright. California would chew him up." Kimberly retrieved a milk jug from the refrigerator and poured some into her cup, turning the brown water into a muddy beige." She used a spoon for fishing out one of her long brown hairs from the cup.

"Plus, they know he's a bum. That's why they don't want him."

"Don't say that. It's not nice. He's family. Now tell me about demolitions school."

"You don't want to hear about that."
"No. But I want to hear you talk..."
***
John pulled up to the curb at the Keating house. Before he could put his pickup truck into park, Ellie was at the passenger door. He leaned over and opened it for her and she jumped in and unzipped her jacket, revealing a paper-thin white blouse.

She drew a deep breath, leaned over to him, and their lips met. They breathed deep from each other's desire.

They parted. Dashboard lights cast soft red light across her face and shined gently through her brown hair. He said, "Ellie, I'm glad you came."

"You came here." She giggled.

"I did."

He leaned in to put an arm around her.

She took his hand off her shoulder and held it in both her hands, fingers intertwined, and pressed to her narrow waist.

He loved her though he'd convinced himself to let her go. He'd been gone since the middle of winter and had seen her only a couple times in the previous two weeks. Before that, since January, he read her words in Facebook messages, and they'd spoken on the phone about their own families and hopes for the future. He'd enjoyed her dreams and wanted to be a part of it. He'd planned and hoped for the next phase of their future to start in a year after he had some time in the Army and picked up some more skills and trades.

He'd graduated half a year behind his friends in high school and they'd all gone their different paths. Only Ellie remained. About a year behind him, she'd just finished summer school and got her diploma early by taking extra classes.

"Look at you, Ellie."

She sat back, "What?"

"Look at you. You are so beautiful. I've loved you since I met you… when?"

"You know when."

"You were a freshman, and I was a junior?"

"Close enough."

He fretted about his late graduation but knew she'd done the same, a little faster perhaps. He tried to forget the school moves and his jobs that took time away from studying. He wanted to forget everything in his past except her. He longed to recall every moment he'd spent with Ellie.

Come to me," he leaned forward.

She said, "Not here. My parents might be watching from the window. Let's go to the warehouse parking lot. The cops never look there. If we turn off the engine and the lights…"

John drove, his hand pressed into her blouse, warm, and feeling warmer. She turned his hand and raised it to her bosom. A sigh escaped her.

He drove.

***

He parked the truck and doused the lights.

Ellie slipped off her flats and turned to John. Their lips met once more.

He unbuttoned his shirt.

Her hands found his chest.

He deftly unbuttoned her blouse with one hand, the other hand pressed to the small of her back as he turned and held her willing body.

John watched her. He saw everything about her. Her head tilted, her lips opened, her long eyelids closed and opened slowly, stopping half-way, and then closing again.

Their warm breath came in gentle waves, synchronized, commingling, carrying desire, want, need.

He pushed her blouse off her shoulders. Her bra was lace and revealing. He unhooked it with expert fingers.

She smiled.

He knew she wanted his fingers and more.

She shrugged off the bra and shifted out of her blouse and set them on the dashboard.

His eyes on her body, John whispered, "Perfect."

"I am?" she pulled back.

"You are." He followed her movement.

She put a hand on his chest.

"Too perfect?"

"Yes."

"Then maybe I shouldn't." She bit her lip, holding the pink flesh in her white teeth.

"You should."

"Maybe not."

"You would entice me to something and take it away?"

"Am I worth more than a throw in a pickup truck?"

"You are worth more than the world."

"Would you give me the world?"

"I'll give you all I have, and I am to earn. I give all of me."

"Then I will give all of myself to you."

Chapter 3 Family Apart

John Wilcox carried his duffle bag onto the porch as Devon stepped out of the Expedition and walked along the path, ignoring Dog's barking. Devon Simmons' brother, Thom, and Kristian 'Paver' Pavilions stayed in the car.

"Wilcox!" Devon called.

John Wilcox said, "Hey, Devon. Thanks for giving me a lift."

"No problem." Devon, standing a head taller than Wilcox, grabbed his friend's bag.

Wilcox said, "It's good to have a giant on the squad."

Devon grinned down. "Or a bunch of midgets."

Dog continued barking at the guests.

"Dog, stop." Wilcox spat a stream of tobacco juice towards Dog, intentionally missing it. It tucked its tail and retreated to the backyard.

"I don't know what's wrong with him." Wilcox offered a hand. "I think Beau's been kicking him. He never used to be so skittish. I could spit right between his front legs, never got a drop on him and he wouldn't flinch."

They shook.

Devon said, "Probably never seen a black guy before."

"Naw... Well, maybe," John said. "I still think that idiot is kicking it."

The screen door slammed as Kimberly Wilcox walked out onto the porch. She was followed by Danny, Samantha – getting tall at twelve-years-old, and Janine, the youngest child, and the family's half-sister at five-years-old. Beau came last, drinking a beer.

"I should have poured them out." Wilcox thought of the beers he'd left in the fridge.

The group walked down to the car, and all of them shook hands with Devon, except for Beau who stood in the back. They waved to Thom who got out long enough to change seats, and to Paver, who stood beside the car smiling and adjusting his hat.

Kimberly hugged her son. "Johnny, be safe." She kissed him on the cheek.

"I will," he said.

"I love you." Tears formed.

"I love you too."

"You are going to drive safe," she said to Devon.

"Yes, Ma'am." His eyes widened, and his cheeks puffed into a smile.

"No question asked. You are going to drive safely. Go. Get out of here."

Wilcox said, "I'll be back in six months or a year, maybe sooner."

"Break a leg." Danny gazed at his brother with admiration.

"Break a leg, Danny." Wilcox put his duffle bag in the trunk of the car and climbed into the back seat, sitting next to Paver who jumped in the other side.

"Hey man," Paver said, putting his fist out.

Wilcox bumped knuckles and said, "Hey."

As Wilcox rolled the windows down and his family waved, he raised a hand. Amid the 'Goodbyes' of his sisters and his mother, plus the machine gunned 'Adios,' 'Later alligator,' and, 'Break an arm,' from Danny, he heard Beau mutter, "Damn niggers."

Wilcox sighed, wishing he'd thrown Beau out of the house his first night back from 12B training.

***

Devon Simmons drove toward Little Rock, listening to the radio with Wilcox, beside him, and Thom and Paver in the back.

Music on the radio stopped in mid-chorus for the station's news lead.

"Breaking news. Fort Smith police are forming riot-squads to disperse protestors when activities turned violent this morning."

Sirens echoed. Devon instinctively looked in the rear-view mirror before realizing it came from the radio. He laughed, and Thom said, "You thought it was us?"

Devon grunted.

"...three days of peaceful demonstrations suddenly

turned as fires set after midnight continue to burn. Firefighters called in departments from the entire region. From this rooftop location burning cars can be seen for miles and businesses are either a blazing inferno or smoldering ruins. Looting started at first light when the chaos exploded. Employees have been instructed by the major corporations to stay home."

"Shit," Devon said.

"They were asking for it. Whoever heard of World Protest Week?" Paver fiddled with his cell phone, watching a video.

"Turn that off. I want to hear this." Devon waved at Paver and increased the radio volume.

"...what started as a peace march and demonstrations at the site of murder last week became fueled by disparate groups protesting for other causes. More protesters arrived yesterday to demonstrate against the current protesters, and police were brought in to keep the groups separate. There are immigration reform groups, police brutality protesters, education demonstrators, abortion activists, religious groups, neo-Nazis, KKK, patriot-militia groups– unarmed until this morning but we heard gunfire.

"Fighting started late yesterday afternoon as each group struggled for the media spotlight. By midnight most of the demonstrations ended, but cars were burned in the early morning, starting with parked and unattended police and emergency response vehicles. I can see an ambulance on fire below us..."

"Jesus, Devon." Thom lit a cigarette. "Is that where you're going?"

"That's a police problem, not the Army." Devon rolled down the window, grabbed the cigarette out of Thom's mouth, and threw it out. "Not in the car. You better not smoke in my car."

Thom reached out too late to get his cigarette back. "You won't be here. You won't care."

Devon said, "If you're driving my car for the next year, you better take care of it, or I'll keep the keys, and you can hitchhike back to Camden."

"Sounds like bullshit to me," Paver removed his clean new camouflage hat and rubbed his short brown hair.

"No Bullshit. No smoking."

"No. Bullshit in the Fort Smith riots. What they need is a healthy dose of .50 caliber." Paver pulled his hat on and set the brim down over his eyes.

"Whatever. Just take care of my ride. We pick up Wilcox, then to the bus stop... And... Thanks for doing this."

***

In Little Rock, the three men climbed onto the bus and took separate rows half-way to the back of the empty bus. A handful of people climbed on and settled in at the very back and front. The bus driver announced the trip from the door, and several more people boarded after stowing their bags underneath.

At a quarter hour past the scheduled departure time, the driver shuffled some paperwork, took his seat, closed the doors, and they departed. There were no conversations of even the pleasant stranger-to-stranger kind.

Buses had evolved and devolved. From rare transportation to friendly passage, to drinking with drunks and lively self-entertainment, to the travel means of the poorest of the poor who needed to go somewhere, and soldiers used buses to go home or report back from leave.

Two hours passed. Paver marked the time from Little Rock.

"And hour-and-a-half left to Saint Louis. Then Uber to Fort Leonard Wood," Paver said from his seat across the aisle from Wilcox. Devon sat beside Paver by the window.

John Wilcox opened a backpack he'd stolen from Beau and hid in his duffle bag. "Demo class wasn't bad. Looking forward to the next set." Reaching into the bag, he retrieved a six-pack, peeled off two beers and handed them to Paver and Devon. "I forgot I had these. They're still a bit cold."

"Damn! Thanks." Devon took the beer and emptied it in one draw.

"Go slow. Two each. I didn't leave all of them for my cousin." John Wilcox's phone rang.

Paver said, "Forget slow. I think the bus driver has us spotted."

Wilcox laughed while struggling with the backpack and retrieving the phone and handing out the second beers.

He answered the call, but before he could speak his mother said, "Johnny, I just wanted to say I love you."

"Love you too, mom," Wilcox replied, dropping his voice, embarrassment creeping in. He wanted to talk to her. He didn't want to speak in front of his friends.

Kim asked, "Did you pack everything you need?"

"Yeah."

"If you forgot anything…"

"I've got everything." Wilcox popped the top on a beer.

"If you did forget...?"

"Mom. I have everything."

"…I could ship it."

"Okay." Wilcox sipped.

"You need to send me your address where you are going," Kimberly said.

"Fort Leonard Wood and after that, I don't know."

"When you do…?"

"Okay."

"Drive safe."

"We aren't driving. We're on a bus." Exasperation filled his voice.

"You know I love you."

"Mom?"

"So you take care."

"Mom?"

"Yes?"

"I need to talk to you." Wilcox lowered his voice. "It's about Beau."

"Yes? What about him? He's your cousin."

Wilcox heard the tension in her words. He reconsidered this conversation, but he'd needed to talk to her. He should have said more about Beau in person the day before, or the weeks before. He hadn't, and he silently accused himself of being a coward for letting his mother's kindness override his intuition. He blurted out, "He's a bum."

"He's your cousin."

"He's lazy."

"He's not lazy."

"Mom... He doesn't..."

"I know that he..."

"He won't keep a job." If she knew, Wilcox thought, why didn't she do something?

"He has problems."

"He's old enough to enlist. The Army would..."

"No dear. Beau's out of shape is all," Kimberly interrupted.

"Physical shape? He'd lose the weight."

"He's slow. Mentally."

"The army will take care of him."

"You know he's an orphan," Kimberly said.

"Dad's sister and her husband have been dead for three years. My dad has been dead for over ten years."

"Don't talk of that."

"You have enough to support. He eats const…"

"Blood is thicker than water."

"He doesn't pull his weight. I think he's been kicking the dog."

"Dog always acts skittish around strangers."

"…Since Beau showed up. Mom. Beau is seventeen. He'll be eighteen in a couple of months. He's not a kid. Time for him to get out on his own."

"Beau's all I have left of my sister."

"You have us—your children. You don't have him. He has you coddling him. He's never going to stand on his own if you keep propping him up."

"I don't coddle him. I couldn't ever put him out."

"Just think about it." He let her off. Beau was messed up, mentally, emotionally, he knew. She should kick him out. Perhaps, he thought, if he'd talked to her at home, but what use was there in arguing now? She and Aunt Claire were as close as sisters before the car accident. With no other family, with dad gone and Kimberly's parents passed, she had no adult companionship. She'd never gone to college and wasn't from Arkansas originally. Her waitressing at the cafe-diner brought her in contact with customers and co-workers. Arkansan people. They would never be true, spit-and-blood friends to an outsider. If they ever did, they'd never admit it to another 'Arkansawyer.' That's what she called herself. Maybe Beau was her only link to the past. Wilcox couldn't bring himself to badger her further. "I gotta go," he said. "I love you."

"Love you too. Drive safe and don't forget the address." She hung up.

She was upset at his words, and he chastised himself for doing that. He wanted to call her back, hesitated, and put the phone away.

He called Ellie. She didn't answer, and he left no message for her. He didn't know what to say. Forced apart by the Army, he still loved her. He hoped she would wait for him, but he couldn't be sure. A high school girl at home with her parents and no college prospects and no money for tuition would be pressured to marry, get pregnant, and raise a family. He'd asked her to join up so they could be stationed together, but she wasn't the military type. She couldn't shoot a gun no matter how many times he'd tried to teach her. She couldn't hunt of fish. She could listen to his worries and complaints. She wanted to be near him, and through high school, they'd spent every spare moment beside each other. She was fun company, and she could make love... He smiled as he thought of the nights they'd spent together, and he grew warm in the memories of her touch, but that would have to wait.

He drew his first beer empty and popped open the other can. The highway disappeared as the road turned into an off-ramp. The bus slowed. The off-ramp ended at a freeway bus terminal and truck stop where the driver pulled the vehicle to a halt at the end of a row of buses. Passengers flooded the pavement, getting onto or off various tour buses, and motor-coaches.

The driver stood up and said, "One more stop and then an open road to Missouri."

Tires squealed. A sedan raced through the parking lot, turning left and right, straightening and turning hard around, aiming for the bus.

The car hit the massive coach in the side, crumpling the luggage bay, wedging itself nearly to the windshield.

An explosion of glass and metal rose in glittering shards. The bus rocked. Wilcox ducked, spilling his beer as the impact shoved him into the aisle.

Chapter 4 Diner

A few minutes after the noontime tornado-test siren finished blowing Kim rushed into the restaurant. She adjusted her work-blouse, having changed clothes in her car.

She called out, "Sorry, Joe."

"You're late." A broad shoulder and round-bellied chef yelled from the host station.

Tammy, the morning shift waitress, blushed and pushed back blonde hairs that had escaped her bun-knot.

"Joe... Five minutes." She sighed and scanned the dining room. Two guests–a couple on a lunch date–looked up.

"I'm docking you for an hour's pay." Joe entered the swinging door to the kitchen.

"At my rate?" Kim hustled around the much younger woman to look at the lunch menu. The food changed daily, and she was expected to know it.

Joe pushed through the swinging door, looked out, and then retreated. "And giving it to Tammy."

Kim said, "She can buy a new car."

Tammy snickered.

"I heard that." Joe stuck his head through the serving counter window.

"No, you didn't."

Joe smiled at the two women. "But I heard the sarcasm."

Kim knew he wouldn't dock her pay. Joe liked to play tough. She said to Tammy, "I had to see my son off. He's heading back to the Army. I skipped the bakery job this morning. Made breakfast for the whole family and still barely made it here."

"Don't worry! I'd do the same thing."

Tammy put her hand on Kim's arm. "Have a good afternoon. I'd say 'great,' but save that for the weekends."

"You too." Kim smiled at Tammy's comment. Kim never took a weekend off.

The front door slammed as a big man pushed his way into the store; the place seemed too small for him. He stomped across the floor like a king of the slums, wearing a white T-shirt and coveralls. A pack of teenagers and preteens followed like mongrel dogs. Their heads turned, their eyes shifted. They looked this way and that, stopping on each patron for a moment as if to decide if the old ladies in the corner or the truck drivers at the counter were predators or prey: An easy mark or too much trouble.

A woman stood outside, clad in a worn and faded flowery dress, as she tied the leash on a mix-breed pit-bull to a signpost. She came through the door, opening it herself, her head down as she meekly and ineffectively herded the last few straggling children.

The big man strode up to Kim and Tammy. "Table for seven."

Tammy said, "We can't..."

Kim cut in, "Mr. Galliger? We can help you. Would you like a booth or a table by the window?"

Greg Galliger said, "Booth, and pull up some chairs."

Kim gathered a handful of menus and led the group across the room until the big man took a seat at a table. His contingent followed and climbed onto the benches and scraped chairs across the floor.

Kim turned back and handed out the menus. "This will do? I'll bring glasses of water for everyone while you look."

She returned to the host station where Tammy said, "Joe wants us to enforce a dress code."

"Not for lunches and it's barely noon."

"They look a bad kind." Tammy put her hand to her mouth.

Kim spoke softer. "They are… They're Galligers. He's been trouble in town for over twenty years. His name is Greg. The mom is okay-Shelley. She's Shelley. The kids are walking the fence between jobs as criminals or cops."

Tammy snickered. "How do you know?"

"I hear things… The youngest girl goes to school with my Sammy. The oldest boy, umm, Shelton, is eighteen and still in high school. Held back several times. Rumored to…" Kim caught herself. "It's not good to gossip."

"Will you be okay with them?"

Kim said, "Go home, Tammy."

"I have to change." Tammy departed for the restroom.

"We're ready to order." Greg, the Galliger patriarch, called over his shoulder.

Kim rushed over with a notepad. "What can I get you?"

"Where're our waters?"

"I've got them coming. What can I get you?"

"They'll all have hamburgers. Medium, with all the toppings. She'll have a salad." Greg flipped his hand toward his wife. "I'll have the prime rib. Got a big job coming in and we're celebrating."

Kim hummed her way through the order, scratching notes with a pencil, and trying to ignore the disrespect the man showed his own family.

Shelton interrupted his father, "I want my burger rare."

"Y'all get it the way I order it."

"I-I-I want it rare."

Kim watched the boy. His eyes had sunk into dark circles caused by much-rumored drug and alcohol abuse, lack of sleep, and poor nutrition.

Greg ignored Shelton. "I'll have a beer. The missus

will have a hot cup of tea, and we want extra bread and butter for the table. And jelly. Bring jelly."

"Right up." Kim turned and retreated to the kitchen to place the order and escape the presence of abuse. She returned to the table with seven glasses of water and a basket of bread and butter, all balanced on a tray.

"More bread," Greg demanded.

Kim finished distributing the glasses. "Right away."

Shelton complained, "I want my-my burger ra-ra-raw."

Greg said, "Raw? Boy, don't be stupid."

"I sa-sa-said raw."

"Y'all said rare, now say raw?"

"I kn-know what-what-what I said."

"No one eats hamburger raw."

Shelley Galliger said, "The French do. It's tartare."

The entire table of children looked at their mother. Greg's mouth opened, speechless.

The woman dropped her head and fidgeted with her dinnerware. She seemed as astounded as everyone else that she'd spoken above her defined place, set by Greg.

Heads and eyes turned from Shelton to Greg to Shelley and back.

Several young voices whispered, "Oh. No," and "Momma?" and "She's gonna get it."

Kim returned to the kitchen and continued to listen to the rising tone of the conversation through the serving window.

"I said, I want raw." Shelton's voice rose.

"Ya ain't so big I can't whoop ya. Y'all get medium and like it. What kind of stupid are ya asking for rare and then asking for raw?"

"I ain't st-stupid."

"Ya sound stupid. Where'd ya get that stutter? Stop talking and stop stuttering. Ya ain't stupid, but ya sounding stupid. Raw hamburger... Jesus-Christ-My-Savior."

"I ain stu...stu....stu..."

"Ya can't even say, 'stupid.' "

"I-I-I ain... arg."

A crash rose from their table.

Kim looked out the serving window as Joe cooked the burgers and steak on the grill. She called out, "Joe."

The chef ignored her.

"Joe? Joe!"

"What?"

"We got a problem."

Joe sprinted around the cook station in time to see Shelton tip the table over on his father and siblings who were trapped by the booth-benches. Water glasses flew. Greg climbed out from under the table, shoving his youngest kids onto the floor as he grappled with Shelton.

Greg yelled at the boys to jump in. They all watched.

"Call the police," Joe yelled. He grabbed a baseball bat from a corner and skittered sideways into the dining room. He held the bat high, ready to swing.

Kim grabbed the wall phone and dialed 911. When the operator answered, she asked for the police. They put her on hold.

The fight moved into the aisle between tables where Shelton pinned his father down and repeatedly punched him in the face. Joe used the baseball bat as a ram to push Shelton off the man.

Shelton slipped off to the side, and both the boy and father struggled to their feet.

"You leave my boy alone," Greg yelled at Joe.

"I'm not having this in my place. You all are paying for any damage."

"I ain't paying for anything." Greg moved into Joe's face as the chef took a step back and raised the bat.

Shelton gained his feet and ducked past his father, decked Joe and toppled him onto another table. It tipped, and they crashed to the floor. The bat flew from Joe's hands.

Shelton climbed over Joe. Landing blows to his face; he gave the cook a beating worse than he'd done to his father. All the Galliger's children joined in to attack Joe with kicks and punches. Shelley stood back, holding her husband's arm, watching, and smiling. Greg too watched and waited, ready to join the fight.

Kim asked 911, "Send the police as quickly as you can." She dropped the phone, padded to her purse at the host station, and withdrew her snub-nose revolver. She held her arm straight down, pointing the gun at the floor, ready to lift it and fire.

She said, "That's enough."

They ignored her.

Kim raised her voice. "Stop. Now. I'm going to shoot someone." She slowly brought the handgun up and repeated her command.

Everyone in the diner froze, except for Shelton who continued to beat on Joe.

"Stop him." Kim waved the gun at Greg. Kim shook her head, trying to clear the ringing in her ears. She realized that Tammy had emerged from the restroom and stood in the corner, screaming like a siren.

Kim called, "Tammy! Tammy!"

The woman fell silent.

Greg looked at Tammy, then to his sons, and back to Kim and the gun. He reached down and grabbed Shelton in a bear hug from behind, pulling the boy from Joe's chest.

Shelton kicked and screamed, replacing Tammy's high wail with low gargles and grunts.

Joe scampered back and away, escaping and reaching

for a bat he kept behind the countre. He struggled to open his eyes. Bruises began to swell on his cheeks and brow.

Two police officers came through the front door with a bang.

Kim lowered the handgun.

The tallest officer put a hand on his holstered gun. "What's going on here?"

Kim put her handgun in her purse as she told the officer's about the fight, while Shelton continued to struggle against his father's wrist-locked hold.

"Sir. You need to stop," the second officer spoke to Shelton. "Did he do this?" He waved the business end of a Tazer at the turned over tables.

"No," Greg said.

"Yes," Joe and Kim replied in unison.

"He done give you that shiner?"

Joe worked his way to his knees and then onto a chair. He touched his eye socket and winched. "Yeah."

"How about you?" The policeman asked of Greg, who still struggled with the boy.

"No. He ain't done nothing. They started it." Greg threw his head towards Joe and Kim.

"Okay. Okay. Let him go," said the taller officer.

"Not a good idea... Boy. You better cut this crap out," Greg said. Greg pushed his son away, releasing him.

Shelton took two steps forward, his head lowered and turned. With fists clenched, he lunged at the officers.

The smaller officer was ready. He aimed and fired. Shelton fell in a heap under the debilitating impulse of the taser.

Before Shelton could recover, and between repeated pulses of the Taser, the taller officer put handcuffs and leg shackles on the boy.

"We're going to take him until he calms down and

then we'll see if any charges get filed."

Greg stepped forward. "You ain't…"

"Stand down, sir." The second officer held the Tazer on the boy but drew his sidearm with his other hand.

Greg bowed to caution and backed off.

The officers hoisted Shelton by the crook of his elbows and dragged him to the parking lot. The family followed.

"Do you need an ambulance?" Kim asked Joe.

"No." Joe winced again. "Do you? You don't look good."

"Thanks."

"Are you sick?" Tammy asked, appearing at her side. The girl's entire body shivered.

"With worry. You look worse than me." Kim gave a nervous laugh.

Tammy said, "You look pretty bad."

Kim shuddered, realizing she'd drawn her handgun for protection, and why. "Joe. Let's get some ice on those bruises. And you," Kim said to Greg. "Get out here and don't you come back."

Chapter 5 The Bus

Wilcox recovered his feet and brushed beer from his drenched OD T-shirt. He helped an old man get back into his seat and asked, "Are you okay?"

The older man nodded. "Is every else okay?"

The bus driver unfastened his seatbelt. "What the hell?" He opened the door and stomped down the steps.

"My God. Look at that," Paver yelled.

The sound of shredding nylon and growls came from the car as the driver tore the airbag with long fingernails. The woman stopped, sat back, and stared at her spectators. Dark blood flowed from cuts on her face and poured down her cheeks to join a stream gushing from her nose and mouth.

"Call 911." A bald, gray-bearded man at the back of the bus moved up the aisle, stepping over fallen bags.

"On the phone with them. 911 is asking about injuries," a reply came from a young stringy-haired, tank-top-wearing-man. "Are there any injuries?"

The bus driver approached the car and leaned in the window. "What the hell are you doing!?" He said, "You could have killed someone... Hey? Are you all right?"

The woman stared at him, grunting, deep and throaty in short bursts.

"Hey. I'm talking to you," said the bus driver.

She cocked her head as if she couldn't see, listening for his voice.

The bus driver reached for the door handle when she lashed, wild grasps of her hands, long slender fingers tipped with long nails hooked into his arm, tearing into his flesh. She pulled him into the car.

He yelled, drawing back, half in the car, half off his feet, but her hands held with inhuman strength.

Teeth sank into the bus driver's arm. She grasped his hair and pulled him entirely into the car. Teeth bite into his nose as she shook her head like a coyote with a rodent. Her next bite went into the neck. His jugular vein burst, and blood filled the car.

She pushed the driver out the window, his shaking and crumpled body falling to the ground. She screeched at Wilcox, Paver, Devon and the others as she climbed onto the hood.

"Get out, get out," someone yelled. The passengers panicked. Thirty people rushed towards the front, falling in the aisle to be stepped on by those people behind. Everyone tried to get down the steps and run away.

"No." Wilcox pointed. "Don't!"

The doors of the bus terminal lobby and ticketing area flew open as people ran out. A man struggled to escape the grasp of another man who crouched and ran like an ape, one hand holding the first man's shirt, tearing the material. The ape-man turned his head to the sky, and bared his teeth, before leaping, biting his victim in the neck. They two staggered and fell with the attacker taking bite after bite of his victim.

Another person crashed through the glass, falling in a heap, sliced in a thousand places from the glass. As soon as he stood up, four men, walking on all-fours, circling like wolves, surrounded him. Snorts filled the air as they caught the scent of blood. Saliva drooled down their chins.

The largest one grabbed an arm and licked at the blood, grunting and prancing in a circle, dragging the victim as a child drags a doll. The others leapt, pinning the dying man down. They pulled on his arms and legs. The tearing of flesh rose in dismemberment. Each wolf-man feasted on an arm or leg.

Wilcox wished for a weapon as he looked at Devon and Paver. "They're insane."

"Look," Devon said. Across the parking lot, a swarm of bloodied people streamed off a bus. They walked in a herd towards the terminal building, but as people escaped through the doors of the convenience store, the people from the bus crouched, sniffed, snorted, and sprinted with flailing arms and staggering legs. The bloodstained mass surrounded people, pouncing on them as the wolf-men had done eating people alive.

"Shit," Paver said. "Get back on the bus." He called to the people still getting off, jumping down the steps into the middle of the carnage. Some turned and tried to get back on, to be pushed out by others getting off the bus, or pulled by their ankles, a grasped wrist, or a caught blouse, yanked into waiting claws and gnashing teeth.

"Drive. Someone drive." Wilcox pushed to the front of the bus, stumbled over people who had fallen. Unable to stop and help them up, he yelled, "I'm sorry. Wait. Stop pushing."

The passengers ignored him as they moved to escape the wild-woman who'd killed the bus-driver, blind to the slaughter around them.

Wilcox reached the front of the bus and slipped into the driver's seat. He started the engine and shifted it into gear. With the gas pedal jammed down, the bus lurched. He pressed the button to close the doors. Some people became trapped by a sliding door, and the mechanism stopped, pinning, and catching a man.

Three people on the steps yelled at the same time, "Open the door," "He's trapped," and, "Let's us out,"

The last one came from a black haired, dark-make-up girl.

He pointed out the window. Adrenaline narrowed his vision. Forcing himself to scan the area, turning his head left and right, he looked for an open path for the bus. He said, "Sit down if you want to live."

"I want to get off...," she protested

"Those people are being murdered. I'm getting us the fuck out of here." He spun the wheel to get out of the line of buses and drive free of the car wedged into its side. The car's driver screeched as the bus pulled and jerked, shaking the car, but not affecting her balance. She moved with the action, standing as steady as a surfer. Her head turned side to side, searching for new victims inside the coach.

The bus jumped, dragging the car with it as Wilcox stepped harder on the gas. Metal tore against metal and the two vehicles separated, but the woman leaped onto the side of the bus. Wilcox swerved, turning left and right, trying to shake her off as she edges towards a broken window with clawing hands and bare feet, toes curled.

"Get her off. She's going for a window," Wilcox yelled to Devon and Paver.

Passengers cowered, moving away from the middle of the bus, pressing themselves into seats. The woman hung from the bus and clawed her way along. Her fingertips and nails ripped into broken steel. She disregarded her injuries.

Wilcox steered the bus across the parking lot. The hordes of beast-people running in random directions turned to the sound, stopping to change course and then charging at the vehicle. Wilcox accelerated, running over several of the creatures.

"You killed them," Paver said. "You murdered those people."

"They aren't people," Wilcox replied.

"No. No. You killed those people." Paver grabbed at his hat, taking it off and putting it back on again.

"Those things aren't people. They used to be people."

"Wha… What?" He took his hat off again and waved it.

"Does that man look like a man?" He pointed at one of the four-limbed creatures wearing human clothing. He ran it over.

"Huh?" Paver jammed his hat on and clung to a seat back and handrail, scanning, and watching the carnage.

"You ever saw a woman run a car into a bus? Drag a man into her car? Eat his arm? Leap onto the hood through the broken windshield? Climb a moving bus?"

"She's getting inside," Devon said. He hammered a fire extinguisher at her hands as she reached the broken window.

An air-horn blew. Looking up from the mirrors,

Wilcox watched a semi tractor-trailer truck on the highway entrance ramp and heading in the wrong direction. Two people in the cab fought for control. The passenger thrashed at the driver who fought off the attack with one hand while attempting to steer with the other. The whites of the trucker's eyes shined when he saw the bus.

Wilcox swerved to the right, putting the bus into a fishtail. The truck driver jammed the wheel around, and the trailer skidded sideways, tires hopping on locked brakes. The two vehicles swiped each other. The trailer pancaked the woman-creature against the bus, breaking all the windows, squashing her, spinning her body, and dropping her to the pavement.

The impact threw Paver, Devon and other passengers to the side.

Wilcox righted the wheel again, over-steered to avoid a concrete barrier, and the bus tipped. Wilcox whipped the steering wheel the opposite direction, and the bus righted itself, landing hard on the tires with a thump, and tipped the other way, rising, heaving, rolling, and plunging onto its side in a shower of glass and debris.

Sparks flew as the bus slid on the concrete.

Wilcox fell. He slammed his arms as he put his palms and forearms out to break the impact. He banged his head into the shards of metal and concrete that continued under the moving bus, kicking debris into his face.

He looked for a way up and out as the roadway ran past, inches from his face. He picked himself up and steadied himself on the shaking and rocking side of the bus. Sparks burned. Smoke rose.

He reached for an arm-rest and stretched to put a vice-like hold on the steering wheel. He pulled himself up as the door beneath him vaporized on the moving concrete, threatening to skin him and grind his bones to dust.

The bus stopped. The noise stopped. The impact had tossed everyone into a stupor. Groans and whines rose. Emo cursed.

Graybeard said, "What the fuck? Where'd you learn to drive?" He rubbed a bloody knot on his head.

Wilcox put his feet down. They stood on broken glass and ground the material into powder from the adrenaline that surged through him. Devon and Paver righted themselves and glared at Wilcox from across rows of seats. The aisle was on the left, unusable. The ceiling formed a wall on their right.

"You trying to kill us?" Paver said as he climbed around and over rows of seats.

"The truck came right at us. Didn't you see it?" Wilcox asked.

Both men shook their heads.

"Help the others," Wilcox said.

"What about the woman who...?" Devon asked.

"Gone. Hamburger," Wilcox said.

"911 is giving me a busy signal," Emo said as she poked her head up. A bloodied lip smudged her black lipstick, smearing the paint on her chin.

"How do we get out of here? The door is down." Devon asked.

"The roof hatch." Wilcox indicated the row of fiberglass overhead doors, now horizontal at shoulder level, marked with 'Emergency Exit.'

Wilcox popped a latch and climbed out. A quarter of a mile up the highway, the carnage at the bus stop continued. They were isolated and safe for the moment.

After opening a half-dozen hatches along the bus's roof, the men worked to help people get out. They climbed over the sides of seats, and walked on the broken windows, stepping on the asphalt where the glass was a moment before. They picked up carry-on bags, laptop cases, passing them out the hatches to be piled up.

"Where's my suitcase?" a woman asked.

"Yeah. I have a briefcase. I don't see it. I gotta go back in," Graybeard said as he riffled through the belongings.

Wilcox put out a hand and said, "The luggage bay is trapped under the side. Paver," he called into the bus. "Hand out the rest of the bags and grab a first aid kit if you see one." To the passengers, he said, "You aren't getting stowed luggage soon or... ever."

The tractor-trailer truck had gone into a ditch and came to a stop. The truck driver jumped from the cab and ran away, followed by his passenger who leapt like a puma, landing on all fours. It sprinted after the trucker with the bounding gait of a predatory animal, one or both hands on the ground with each stride. Palms flat on the pavement, fingertips curled as it launched itself forward.

Standing too far away to help the trucker, Wilcox said, "Cars. We need a car."

Sparse highway traffic passed by, oblivious to a world going crazy.

"No one is going to stop for us, not with a bus terminal right there," Devon said.

"We gotta go," Paver said.

"Where?" Wilcox asked. "That's not some riot like in Fort Smith. Those people are..."

"What?" Paver asked. "What are they?"

"Insane..."

"We gotta report for duty. They'll declare us AWOL."

"That's two hundred miles. You gonna hitchhike?" Wilcox asked.

Horns blew as a car crossed the grass median, sending dirt and debris sailing into the air. It plowed through the drainage swale by the big rig. The vehicle became airborne as it crossed into oncoming traffic, and careened, swerving and veering up the highway. The bus passengers ran for the safety of the woods. The three soldiers joined them. The car hit a light pole and burst into flames.

In its wake, more cars crashed, hitting guard rails, trees, spinning, and burning. An explosion rose.

"Those people need help," Wilcox yelled as he chased after the others.

"We need help," a woman said.

Wilcox stopped in the woods as they all looked back. The woman was short-statured, middle-aged, and correct. They all needed help. Something weird was going on. People had turned on each other. People turned into animals. But these people were safe. They were his people. He would protect them if he could. Out there, he thought, people were being killed in car accidents, or assaulted with bare hands and bared teeth. Those things used cars as weapons. Weapons. They needed weapons.

Wilcox asked, "What's your name?"

"April." Her eyes widened behind dirty brown hair.

"April. Hello. Will you find anything we can use as weapons."

"I'm on it." She ran back to the bus.

"And first aid kits," Wilcox added. "Check around the driver's seat."

"Weapons? Do we gotta kill these people?" Emo asked.

"They aren't people anymore."

"Cool," she said.

"What about the people in the cars?" Devon asked.

"That's what the first aid kit is for."

Sirens rose in the distance. Police cars and ambulances pulled into the rest-stop. Then a dozen fire engines arrived.

"Weapons." Paver adjusted his hat and looked at the

others.

Wilcox and Devon ran towards the first police car as the officer got out of the car.

"I called it first." Paver hollered and ran after them.

The officer stood staring, wild-eyed, watching them approach. He drew his handgun and fired randomly in their direction. His partner climbed out the other side with a shotgun. The shotgun discharged, not aimed at anyone, not hitting anyone.

"Shit," Wilcox said as he dropped into a crouch and turned twisted, making himself a smaller target.

A randomly fired bullet sung past Devon's head. "Fuck! Always shooting at the black guy, eh?"

The three men returned to the woods at a sprint.

From the safety of the trees, they watched the officers turn toward the crashed cars, firing and reloading. They seemed to take better aim as they attempted to kill drivers and spectators.

A man standing beside his wrecked car, steam billowing from the vehicle's broken radiator, waved his hands. He caught a blast of pellets to the chest. Blood filled the air, and he sprawled over his dented hood.

Paver pointed to the overturned motorcoach. "Back to the bus. The roof and floor will stop bullets," Paver said.

"Nothing here is safe. We gotta leave," Wilcox said.

"But? What's going on?" April asked as she arrived with a first-aid kit in hand.

"It's the apocalypse," the emo-girl said. "Geez."

"Hey. Girl?" Wilcox raised his hand to put on her shoulder.

She squirmed away. "Don't touch me."

"Sorry. What's your name?"

"Stevie." Her eyes gazed down.

"Stevie. I'm John. They call me, 'Wilcox.' Private

First Class. That's PFC Paver, and he's PFC Devon. We're going to get out of here." He scanned the group, the road, and the woods. "We're going someplace, but we'll be okay. This is some crazy riot. It'll end soon? Okay?"

He lied. It was more than a riot, but they nodded. He used deceit for the sake of those few people who might suffer a mental breakdown over the end-of-the-world.

Greybeard said, "You guys are Army, so I'm with you. Gerald Sikes. Desert Storm. I used to come through here all the time. There's a farm-supply store. They have guns, hardware, weapons..."

"Let's go there." Wilcox took another look at the truck stop.

The police officers continued to shoot, sometimes hitting people, including a firefighter among a group of first responders. The man's companions grabbed him, and under a barrage, retreated to their truck and drove away.

A group of attackers, killing people with claw-like hands and gaping maws pounced on cars that stopped, smashing windshields with fists to get at the people inside. Drivers who didn't stop, instead, accelerated, running down attackers and victims at random.

They moved deeper into the woods, following Gerald.

"Shit," said the Tank-Top.

"What's your name?" Wilcox asked.

"Why?"

"Come on, man... I'm going to call you Tank-Top," "Okay."

Wilcox turned to a clean-shaven man. "Who are you?"

"Tim."

"What are you good at?"

"Nothing."

Wilcox grimaced. "I hope not."

"I'm Barry," a bald man said.

"How about you?" Wilcox said to a short-statured man.

"Chuck." The man's barrel chest heaved with the effort.

"Okay. Everyone knows each other. Let's try to keep everyone alive and go find some weapons."

Gerald hurried, and the other's picked up their steps through the brush.

Paver walked beside Wilcox. Paver took his camouflaged lid off and put it back on. "What are we doing?"

"Heading for safety," Wilcox said.

"I mean after that."

"I'm going to call Ellie. I'm going to call home. You should do the same."

"Yeah."

"Then we call Fort Leonard Wood and tell them we aren't going to make it by tonight."

"Or ever," Devon said.

Wilcox weighed the truth of those words. They might never get there.

The dozen bus passengers moved through sparse woods and came to a utility road which they followed to a paved road.

Gerald said, "Branson."

They walked through a quiet neighborhood.

Tank-Top, "Let's steal a ride."

The others ignored him.

Deserted streets greeted them where one expected a few cars, kids on bicycles, a yard-sale, or someone texting and jogging.

A tow-truck approached at high speed. It passed at a roar. The driver stared straight ahead.

"Where are we?" Paver asked.

"Branson," Gerald replied.

Someone peered from behind the window-blinds of a house.

The group left the neighborhood behind. They came to the main street.

As noise rose from a farm supply store, a half-dozen vehicles pulled into the parking lot across the street. Passengers yelled as they ran into the store. "They're coming. They're coming."

Wilcox trotted across the street with the group following.

A man getting out of his car hefted a shotgun. "You better get inside. The zombies just took out the school."

"Zombies?" Wilcox asked.

The man pointed.

The group stopped and looked back.

A mass of people moved up the road in a tangled, disjoined mob. Some ran to houses and stores while others walked. The rumble of a thousand growling voices rose over the sound of breaking glass and car alarms. Gunshots echoed from a gun-store along the block. Ahead of the horde, people ran to their cars, climbed inside, and sped away, passing the group. The people looked out with arched eyebrows, gaping mouths, and flushed skin.

Clouds of dust and exhaust trailed each vehicle.

Wilcox said, "Let's take a car."

"For all of us?" Devon said.

Wilcox counted nine members in the group. They'd lost a few people from the bus. Probably, they'd left on their own. "Nine. We'll need more than one car."

"Wilcox? They're coming fast." Devon moved towards the store.

"We gotta get weapons." Paver ran, and everyone followed.

Gerald said, "We'll bar the doors."

At the storefront, after Wilcox let the other people pass him by, he reached and pulled on the steel roll-up doors that secured the building during off hours.

People pushed shopping carts of looted supplies under the doors, escaping the store.

"Get back inside," Wilcox yelled.

They ignored him. The thieves loaded chainsaws, lawnmowers, and discount TVs into cars.

The attackers entered the parking lot and raced towards the looters. Too late to run, too late to drive away, everyone outside became swarmed. Bashed with fists, ripped open by bare hands, clubbed with stones, torn by teeth, no one lived for long. Screams mixed with the shredding of flesh soon drowned and fell beneath a torrent of guttural ecstasy of killing.

Wilcox started to lower the second roll-up door.

A voice yelled, "Let me out."

He turned to find a store employee pushing a cart filled with food.

"Let me out." The teenage employee said.

Wilcox said, "You want to go out there?"

"Yeah."

"Look."

The teen peered outside.

Three once-human creatures tackled a man running toward the store. His torso swung, thrown side-to-side, pulled left and right amid screams. Tearing of cloth and flesh rose as his arms were violently detached.

The boy's jaw hung. "Close it. Close it."

Wilcox rolled down the security door, ducking inside as it fell. Unable to latch the door, he stepped on the steel lip.

The boy said, "The doors lock from the outside."

"Devon, hold that other door down."

The big man stepped onto the lip, holding it in place.

Banging fists and scratching claws shook the steel. "Paver, find something to hold these doors closed."

"Let me out. I've got to get home," a woman said from behind a motorized shopping cart, coming to a stop behind the teenager.

"Too late," Wilcox replied. "Stevie, April Tank-Top? Check the back and side doors, close them and lock them."

The shopping cart woman protested. "Who put you in charge? Just cuz you wear Army clothes...."

"They did." He gestured to the rattling door.

Paver carried two pole saws. "We can bar the doors with these. Pile up a bunch of stuff." He handed one to Wilcox.

"Jam the end on the metal edge by my foot and push it up against the ceiling," Wilcox said.

Paver pushed the handle end onto the door and raised the blade, extending it against the drop-ceiling tiles, which shifted and moved.

"Make it longer, go up to the roof," Wilcox said.

Paver extended the handle out to twenty feet and braced it against the roof trusses above the tiles. It stayed.

"Great. Now the other one," Wilcox said.

"Are you going to let me out of here?" Cart-Woman asked.

"Do you want to die?"

"What?"

"There are hundreds of those things out there. People are dying."

"But..."

"Shut up for a second."

"I have to get home."

"We all have to get home, but the front doors are not

the way out."

Stevie ran up, out of breath, and said, "Backdoors closed and locked."

"And you aren't getting out the back doors either," Wilcox said. "Find a weapon, find some food, go get a chair in the lawn and garden area, and take a nap. I don't care what you do, but no one is leaving until I say so." He turned to the others who had gathered around. "Gerald, you said there are guns?"

"Yeah, but the guy won't unlock them."

"What guy?"

"An employee."

"Devon, Paver..." The three soldiers walked to the sporting goods aisle. A geeky teenager and a middle-aged woman stood in front of the gun cases.

"We need those weapons." Wilcox read the nameplate on her smock. "Doreen?"

"Not without a credit card, background check, and paperwork. I have to call for an instant background check."

"Here you go." Wilcox picked up the phone and handed it to her. "Call the police. Call the FBI. Do a background check."

She took the phone and dialed a number. After a moment, she said, "This is Doreen Hill from Atwoods Farm and Feed. Store number? Huh? What?" She paused and listened. "Soldiers want our guns. I can't give them guns. They belong to the..." A faint and nearly intelligible voice came over the phone. Doreen stammered and asked, "Give them to them? Hello? Hello? He hung up." She lowered the phone.

Wilcox smiled.

"What did he say?" Devon laughed.

"He said to give you the guns."

Wilcox said, "Then give us the guns."

"I have to call my manager." Doreen raised the phone again.

"Call your manager." Paver pushed the woman aside, picked up the cash register, and threw it into the front of the glass case. It shattered.

"Hey!" Doreen yelped, picked up the phone base, stepped back, and dialed again.

Wilcox kicked the glass on the ammunition display case and pulled out boxes of shotgun shells, rifle ammunition, and small caliber pistol rounds while Paver unlocked the longarms and stacked them on the countertop.

"He's not answering the phone." Doreen hung up.

Wilcox stacked ammunition by caliber on the countertop. "No one is answering the phones anywhere. That's not a riot outside. They are...? I don't know what they are, but that's not a riot."

She scoffed.

Wilcox said, "Not funny Doreen."

"You aren't joking?"

"I suggest you grab a gun for yourself."

"I have one."

Wilcox demanded, "Get it out."

She unzipped a fanny pack. Without touching it, she revealed a small frame handgun.

"Good. Keep it handy. Is that a .32?" Wilcox said.

She nodded.

Wilcox handed her a box of ammo. "Find an extra magazine for it. We have a problem." Wilcox scanned the guns in the case.

"That's all?" Devon picked up a box of ammo.

Wilcox read off the weapon models and calibers. "Three AR-15s in .308 and .223, two Ruger .22 semi-autos, two 12 gauge shotguns, and two deer rifles–one .308 and a 30-06. That's two or three boxes of ammo per gun maximum."

"Some of these calibers don't go with those guns," Devon said.

Wilcox said, "I can use the powder out of any ammunition we can't shoot. Doreen? Do you sell reloading supplies?"

"Lots," Doreen replied.

Wilcox said, "I need all the gunpowder, black powder, and bullets you have."

"Bullets?" Devon asked. "If they get in we won't have time for reloading."

"Bullets for shrapnel."

Paver asked, "Make bombs?"

Wilcox nodded. He grabbed binoculars off a shelf and used the box to break the glass on a knife display. He retrieved a hunting knife and scabbard. "Anyone need a knife?"

Screams came from the front of the store.

"Get those guns loaded." Wilcox grabbed a shotgun and jammed four shells into the tube magazine. As he ran with the shotgun hooked under his arm, he stuffed another handful of shells into a pocket.

Chapter 6 Tea Break

Kim entered the back door and set her purse on the counter. "All the lights are on except the one I needed." She turned on the back-porch light because she knew that Beau would be heading out to work soon.

The overhead light in the living room burned along with the lamps on the end tables and a hope-chest. Kim flipped the wall switch and doused all but one table lamp. Her bedroom lights glowed. She wondered if Janine and Samantha had been playing dress-up or experimenting with her makeup again. As she returned to the kitchen and reached through the doorway, she fingered the switch to off.

"They always forget, and they don't know how expensive electricity is… I can forgive them. They are their childhood as they should."

She retrieved her tip-money from the restaurant and counted it out before placing it in an envelope for deposit at the bank first thing in the next morning.

She put bread in the toaster, ran it down, then poured a cup of coffee and microwaved it.

A check of the trash confirmed four frozen dinners had been emptied, presumably consumed by the family. She checked the freezer and noted that she needed to pick up more frozen meals. But for tomorrow, she took frozen green beans and peas. She gathered onions and ground hamburger from the refrigerator. A forty-pound bag of potatoes and the crockpot from the pantry started her dinner preparation for the next night. She seared the beef in chunks in a frying pan, and while monitoring the stove, she chopped the potatoes and onions. Everything plus water and spices went into the crockpot on a low simmer. She set the timer for eight hours.

In the middle of her preparations, the toaster popped. She buttered the slices and plated them. She turned the heat up on the tea kettle and set the coffee cup from the microwave on the table alongside her empty teacup, a Lipton bag inside and the tag wrapped around the handle.

"Do you want a cup of tea?" Kimberly asked her nephew when she heard his stomping gait on the stairs.

"Naw, Auntie." He tromped into the kitchen, saw the coffee cup, and laughed.

"You need it." She returned to the counter to retrieve the buttered toast. "Eat."

"Not hungry. You have some."

"Too tired to eat." She sat down. "I'll nibble... Are the kids in bed?"

Beau sat across from her. "Yes. Sammy is reading a book. Danny is playing a game. Janine begged me to read her a story like John does."

"They miss him. I miss him." Tears welled in her eyes, but she choked down her feelings. "I looked forward all day to sitting down and talking to you. I can't talk to anyone at work. Oh. I'm so tired."

Beau shifted uncomfortably. "You don't have to stay up."

"I miss our talks. I know you have to leave soon. Do you want me to take you to the recycling center tonight?" Eyes sunken from exhaustion revealed she wasn't up for the drive.

"I'll walk. I'm used to it. And I need the exercise."

"You're fine. Don't let anyone tell you differently."

Beau rubbed his ample belly and sipped his coffee. He didn't want to say how much he wanted and desired a ride to work. "You work two jobs, and I hitchhike. Sometimes I get picked up."

"It's five miles."

"I can do it in an hour and a quarter. Sometimes an hour and a half. Most nights, Trey goes by and stops and gives me a lift. Sometimes he doesn't see me in the dark. I know his car with the broken headlight and broken taillight, but that's usually when I'm less than a half mile from the plant."

"But then you have to walk home in the mornings."

"Trey gives me a ride to the county turnoff. That's only a mile or so from here."

"Two."

"Two miles. You know I stop at the minimart sometimes for a beer..."

57

"I wish you wouldn't drink, but with working swing-shift, I can't blame you... How are you doing? Do you like the job?"

He frowned.

"Dumb question." She laughed to hide her guilt when she realized she might have shamed him. She whispered, "Sorry."

"It's okay. Dead-end. In twenty years I can be the foreman... That's what the big boss said last night."

"Ignore him. You'll be fine. Something better will come along. Hey. Let me tell you what happened at the restaurant today..." She relayed the story of the fight.

Chapter 7 Violence For Sale

The pole-saw that held down the right-side security door had fallen, and predators opened the door enough to crawl under it. Gerald, Stevie, Tank-Top, and others smashed skulls with hammers and crowbars before the attackers could stand.

Wilcox jammed the shotgun into Stevie's hands and moved into the fray.

Devon and Paver arrived with AR rifles. Doreen carried her handgun, and the teenagers followed with a shotgun and a crossbow.

Wilcox used his knife to stab them in the head and pulled their dead bodies inside as new flesh-eaters grabbed at the legs of their fallen brethren. They pulled themselves under, riding on his efforts to clear the space and reclose the door. Gerald switched from killing zombies to clearing away bodies, making room to close the doors. The attackers crawled, died, and piled up faster than the defenders could lower the security barrier.

"Shoot through the door. Spray-and-pray." Wilcox yelled.

Devon and Paver fired. Bullets riddled the steel with holes and birdshot splattered back at them.

Wilcox waved off Stevie and the store employee. "Save the shotguns. They're useless on the door. Shoot the ones on the ground in the head."

The bullet-hole-punched beings crawled in, gushing blood. They smeared the purple jell across the floor, making it slick and slippery. Stevie set one foot on the steel lip to hold down the left side security door which was pounded upon and rattled from outside. The pole holding it down threatened to fall. Her other foot, set wide, kept her from falling and with each blast of her shotgun, she swung and swayed, attempting to stay upright.

"Rock salt. Do you have rock salt?" Wilcox called to Doreen.

"No."

"Driveway grit, or potting soil?"

She turned, grabbed a shopping cart, and disappeared into the aisles, returning minutes later with bags of wood shavings marked, 'Livestock bedding.'

She sliced them open with a pocket knife and pulled them apart, turning the bags inside-out in a cloud of dust. She kicked it across the floor. The chips turned black with blood.

"All-y'all," Wilcox yelled to those who watched in horror, unable to turn their eyes away from the carnage. "Get the rest of the ammunition and magazines and load all of them."

"How do we do that?" Someone called.

"Bring it here. I'll show you."

***

They fought for hours, expending every bullet and then resorting to tools from the hardware aisle to break skulls and puncture lungs. Hundreds of the human-beasts pushed under the door, raising it further open. They continued until the doorway filled, and no others could fit.

The battle died. A seven-foot-tall, quivering, twitching pile of bodies filled the space where double glass doors once stood. Corpses quaked in the death-throws of those trapped underneath, crushed by the weight. The sounds of the inexhaustible attacker continued as they pushed on the mass, endlessly, desperately trying to get inside to kill everyone within. A wall of dead blocked them.

Others attackers came at the rear doors, pounding on them with rocks. Teenagers, farmers, and looters trapped in the store with the bus passengers moved to protect the steel doors and keep constant watch.

When the main assault ended, Wilcox said, "Stevie. Good job keeping that other door closed. Hey you? Your turn."

"Huh?" The Tank-Top Kid's eyes glassed over as his arms hung weak, the crowbar in his hands straining his shoulder from hours of bashing heads.

"There's no other way to keep the door closed. You need to stand on the edge. Everyone takes a turn. Guard the door. Keep it closed. We'll rotate. An hour on, everyone works for one hour a day."

"A day? How many days will this…?"

Paver's phone rang. He scrambled to answer it, missed the call as he fumbled with his rifle, then checked the screen. "Don't recognize the number."

Devon's and Wilcox's phones rang.

Wilcox answered.

Someone yelled, "PFC Wilcox?"

Wilcox didn't recognize the voice. "General orders canceled."

"What's going on?" Wilcox asked.

"Get to base ASAP. The president declared martial law

ten minutes ago."

"What about Posse Comitatus?"

"Suspended. We're at war. Get to Fort Leonard Wood immediately." The sound of gunfire came over the phone.

Wilcox said, "That might be…"

"No excuses. Get here." An explosion drowned out the voice.

"Are you under attack?"

"What the fuck do you think?"

Faint hollers came through the phone from a distance. "They're coming. Get ready."

Screams and cries of agony rose in the mix of gunfire.

"Sir? Sir?" The phone went dead.

Devon stood wild-eyed, staring at his phone as a voicemail played.

"Devon?" Wilcox waved his hand in front of the man's eyes.

"Yeah?" He looked up.

Wilcox said, "Call home. Make sure your family is okay."

"Okay. What are we doing?"

"We're going home."

"Okay."

"Do it. Call your wife. Call your family."

"Now?"

"Yes. Now."

"We're going home?"

"You to your home. Me to mine. Paver?"

The man answered, "Yeah?"

"You too."

Devon looked at his phone again and dialed. Wilcox did the same. No one answered.

"Do we get to have guns?" Cart-Woman sat in a lawn chair, playing the spectator to the attack, listening to conversations, and fiddling with games with her phone.

"No. You don't get a gun." Wilcox walked over to her.

"You need to see this." She laughed, raised the volume, and turned the screen for him to see a news-streaming service.

Clouds of smoke rose above a city skyline behind a blonde newswoman. *"Rioting is going on in every major city. Boston reports a dozen buildings on fire and hundreds of people attacked and killed. San Francisco is burning to the ground with hundreds of out-of-control fires and thousands of people dead. All the boroughs of New York report blazes. Hospitals are over capacity with injured. Witnesses claim they barely escaped crazed protestors wielding bats, pipes, and other weapons. Some of the injured said they were bitten and clawed. Protestors are rioting everywhere."*

"Turn it off." Wilcox looked away.

"It's wild." Cart-Woman cackled.

"Turn it off."

"What's the matter?"

"Don't you want to get home? Didn't you say you need to save your husband or someone?" Wilcox hated the way she smiled as if she watched a reality TV show.

"Oh. My family is dead. I called home. No one answered."

"That doesn't mean they are dead. Phone lines can be down. Power could be out. Your family might be okay. We all need to get out and go home."

She laughed louder, and when he stared at her, her face dropped into a stupor, an emptiness of intelligence. He wondered if she had a learning disability.

The longer he spied her flickering eyes and twisting turning head, the more the muscles in his back chilled. He thought she might be psychotic. Had she gone crazy? Was now too soon after combat for PTSD?? Hour after hour of killing, from the bus station to the farm store, recalling his participation, he wondered if his thoughts were crazy, his own actions insane. He thought, "They'd killed hundreds of people... Protestors? No. Not humans. Monsters. Humans who'd lost their higher intelligence, reverting into cave dwellers, Neanderthals, cannibalistic predators. They crept along floors like lions and leaped with the grace of coyotes. Do I doubt my eyes? If this violence subsides and we have laws again, there'll be investigations. How could I kill so many? Is self-defense enough?"

The man in the parking lot had used the word, 'Zombie.' That bothered him. "They aren't the living-dead. They're people who've gone insane. Hunting, killing, and eating like animals. Animals who enjoy the kill. Cart-Woman must agree. We fought for their lives. Well, me and the others fight. Cart-Woman watches."

He returned to the sporting goods aisle and looked for more ammunition, discovering powder and primers for reloading cartridges.

"We don't have time to reload bullets." Stevie clomped her boots as she walked the aisle.

"No. But we can use a few bombs." Wilcox saw Devon and Paver at the end of the aisle. "Are all the doors guarded?"

They nodded.

"Good. I need binoculars and access to the roof. They don't sell dynamite here, do they? Fuses? Detonators?"

Devon shrugged while Paver turned away, scanning signs at the end of the aisles. Stevie slipped away.

Doreen walked up with several boxes of ammunition.

Wilcox said, "Doreen. Will you marry me?"

She said, "Too late. I got a man at home... and you not much older than a boy. I could get divorced, but my husband would divorce me for it." She chortled.

"Where'd you get that?"

"I used to keep the ammo locked up in a safe in my office. We stopped doing that. I thought to check and look at what I found!"

Wilcox said, "If no marriage, and I'll marry you, then we need threaded carbon steel pipe–not galvanized, a drill, plumber's sealant or grease, fuses–if they sell dynamite, matches to make fuses–if they don't, lighters to start the fireworks."

"MacGyver, how about a garage door opener?" Devon asked.

"What for?"

"Remote detonator."

"Good idea. Primers. I can make detonators." Wilcox opened a case of small pistol primers. "That would take too long. Get a hacksaw. We can cut the barrels off a couple .22 handguns. Mount the muzzle to a bomb. Run a wire to the trigger, and that'll fire the charge. They sell wire here? We'll make tripwires and attach them to the triggers." His emotions swung from terror during the attack to survival-based killing, and then to enjoyment in the thought of bomb-making. Related hopes and plans of an escape from the building worked around the edges of his mind.

Filled with adrenaline, he knew he could last for days without sleep, long after his friends dropped in fatigue. "Talk to everyone in the store. Find out what car they drive and if they have the keys handy. We'll blast a hole through the zombies and run for the cars."

Devon squinted. "Get the hell out of town? Then what? Where do we go?"

"Home."

"Your home is closest."

"Did you get a hold of anyone?"

Devon took his phone from a pocket. "No one answers when I get through the busy signal. If the phone rings they don't pick up."

"Could be any reason. Let's get out of here. Go home. See what's going on."

Stevie returned, pushing a carriage filled with tools and lengths of pipe. "The roof access is in the back. There's a ladder up from the loading bay."

Wilcox smiled at her.

She lowered her gaze. Her long black hair drooped to conceal her eyes. She asked, "Are you enjoying killing these things?"

"Scared as all get-out."

She turned. "Me too but having fun. This way." She left the carriage, and the three men followed her through the swinging stockroom doors.

Cart-Woman sat in a lawn chair, guarding the rear door with a crowbar in her hands while the store manager paced the floor. Her electric cart sat beside her. She'd plugged it in to charge it. The woman alternately dialed the store cordless phone and a cell phone. "No answer." She paused as they entered.

"Keep trying," Wilcox said.

Stevie disappeared down a row of tall steel racks loaded with watering troughs, barbeque grills, and portable hen-houses.

Wilcox, Devon, and Tank-Top caught up to her by the ladder, barricaded by boxes and crates.

"You got a habit of disappearing… How'd you know it was here?" Wilcox asked.

"I looked around."

"Nice."

Wilcox jumped on top of the boxes, grabbed a rung, and climbed the ladder. A padlock secured the hatch at the top.

"Bolt-cutters."

Tank-Top returned to the store and retrieved the tool. He climbed several rungs to hand them to Wilcox.

Wilcox held the ladder with one hand and with a leg hooked through the rungs of the ladder, to keep his balance, he carefully gripped and then squeezed the handle of the cutters—the other handle pressed into the crook of his shoulder. The lock snapped.

"Heads up." He dropped the cutters onto the boxes below. He turned the latch and pushed the trapdoor up and open.

As the sun set and darkness grew, the two men climbed onto the flat rooftop. The sounds of growling rose as they approached the front of the building and peered over the edge with binoculars.

Three of the primordial enemy stood in the far corner, away from the central mass, shoulder to shoulder and facing each other. Their lack of movement contrasted with the chaos. That odd difference caught Wilcox's attention. Between the three stationary ones, the humans, or used-to-be humans, fifty yards of asphalt filled with zombies. The creatures walked in circles and jumped on cars. They slammed rocks into the concrete walls and metal-clad doors of the store. Others crouched to paw at white-painted parking lanes, pick at the rubber of tires, or chew windshield wipers. Some lay prone, flat on their backs waving arms and legs in the air. One with a broken leg hopped along. Another with a damaged knee dragged the limb along the ground. Others crawled on hands and knees.

Beyond that mass of insanity, the three standing in a tight circle appeared to be talking, but through the binoculars, Wilcox couldn't see their mouths or heads moving. They stood staring past each other into the distance.

Wilcox said, "In a world of weird, that's different...
Hand me a sniper rifle, and we'll end this right here."

Devon replied, "Gerald has a deer rifle with a scope."

A sedan raced up the road, headlights flashing and
bobbing, and with a squeal of the tires, it turned into the lot.
The brakes locked, sliding to a stop as it plowed over
several zombies. Through the windshield, Wilcox saw the
driver struggle with the shifter. Gears ground metal on
metal. The engine stalled, and the driver restarted it.

In a fluid, synchronized move the three standing in the
corner turned, then every zombie rotated their heads toward
the car, and charged. The ones closest banged on the
vehicle with fists, sticks, and rocks, shattering the driver's
window. Others pushed their way in, shoving in hysteria to
get to the occupants.

The driver fought them with an ice-scrapper. A zombie
grabbed the weapon while another grabbed his arm.

A gunshot rang out, and the zombie fell, releasing its
grasp.

Wilcox ducked his head, shaking it to free the ringing
as he covered his ears. "Damn man. Warn a guy."

"Sorry." Devon leveled his rifle, aiming again with the
muzzle a foot from Wilcox's head. Devon fired several
more rounds, killing the zombies at the driver's door.

The driver shifted the car into reverse and backed over
several zombies, breaking their legs and spines. It reached
the road with zombies running after it. The driver shifted
into first gear and sped away.

The sounds in the parking area diminished with the car
fading into the distance.

"Was that one guy worth four bullets?" Wilcox raised
his binoculars.

"Why are you asking that?"

"I don't know. There's a lot of us, and we've got to get out of here. That guy is gone. Was he worth it?"

Devon lowered his carbine. "Don't ask me that. You're the one going home on leave to hunt and stock up the freezer. Is your family worth it?"

Wilcox said, "Of course."

"Then his family is worth it. What's wrong?"

"I don't know. I... It's all this killing."

Devon patted his rifle like a beloved pet. "That's what we trained for."

Wilcox sighed. "Killing terrorist or Russians. North Koreans. Maybe a few Iranians, but not our people. Not our own people."

"They aren't our people. They're monsters. Like, hiding-under-the-bed, trolls under the bridge monsters, only real. Yeah, that guy was worth four bullets."

"What if four bullets are the difference between you and me getting out, or not?"

"They won't be."

They stood in silence for a long time. The three zombies in the corner returned to their tight circle, communications somehow. A serene quiet came to the area. The zombies stood still, crouched, or sat on cars. A low hum began to fill the night as if the creatures meditated and drifted in and out of sleep.

Wilcox said, "A car is our way out."

"There's a lot of people in this store. We can't all escape," Devon said.

"We're going to try."

"There's enough food here to last for days, maybe weeks."

"So we have time."

"What about the army? National Guard? SWAT?" Devon looked through binoculars, peering over the scene.

Wilcox said, "You know as well as me."

Devon looked up. "What?"

"We have nothing and know less about what's going on. We assume nothing. We're on our own. Us versus them. Our families versus them. My mom, brother, sisters. I'm going home. Your wife and brother. You're going home."

Devon pointed. "There's a U-Haul truck. That could hold a bunch of people."

Wilcox asked, "If it's empty?"

"No guarantee…"

Screams came from below. They turned and ran to the roof hatch.

Wilcox swung onto the ladder, descended quickly. He hopped off the boxes and pulled his handgun. Devon landed beside him, struggling with the rifle slung over his shoulder.

The screams mixed with growls as they rounded the corner by the loading dock. A score of zombies streamed through an open door. Wilcox hit the door with his shoulder, shoving back a zombie. As it slammed closed, he threw the deadbolt.

Stevie and Tank-Top swung hand-axes, slicing at arms, breaking ribs and shoulders as they retreated through the doors to the front of the store. Cart-Woman watched from behind them. The teenagers arrived, killing zombies as they crossed through the double doors. Gerald fired his rifle but hits to the torso didn't stop them. Paver came in swinging a bat, his long-gun looped across his back.

Devon crouched and fired single shots up and into the backs of the zombie's heads, watching the background to avoid collateral damage from bullet over-penetration. Half of them turned back towards the men.

Wilcox stalked and circled behind, taking aim with his

handgun, releasing round after round. Blood splattered the shelves and boxes. Dead zombies bled out on the floor. The gray mass of brains and white skull fragments flew in chunks and globules. When Wilcox's gun clicked, he drew his knife and drove it into their skulls. The last zombie fell from Stevie's blow to its neck.

With all the zombies dead, everyone stared at Wilcox with wide eyes, bearing slack faces, and exhausted arms.

He grew angry. "Shit. Shit. Shit. How'd that door get unlocked? Who let them in? I want an answer."

No one responded.

"The door must never have been locked." Stevie stepped forward.

"You said..." Wilcox glared at her, but she returned the gaze until he dropped his shoulders and rubbed his neck. Realizing that accusing her didn't fix anything–she was a kid–he thought, "No one got hurt, so she gets a pass... due to her age and experience. And who'd ever experienced this before? No one."

He pointed. "Tank-Top, you others... Get these bodies moved. Stack 'em in a corner." He thought that would keep the lot of them busy while he worked on an escape plan. "Please. Let's check all the doors again. Lock them. Barricade them. We all have work to do." He sheathed his knife and started reloading the pistol's magazine.

"How're we getting out of here?" Gerald reloaded the shotgun.

"I'm working on a plan. Doreen? Do you sell explosives or fireworks?"

"No."

"Ever make a bomb?" Wilcox looked at Paver and Devon.

"Never tried."

"I'll show you and Devon, but do as I say and you

won't blow yourselves up. Doreen?"

"Yes, sir?"

Wilcox scanned her blood covered clothing and then looked down at himself and the clothes of the others. He thought that if the zombies come from a blood-borne virus, then everyone in the store is infected. "I need your people to gather supplies. I need Tannerite..."

"What's that?"

"Exploding targets. Got any?"

"Maybe."

"Fertilizer, peroxide, acetone... That's nail polish remover or paint remover, and car batteries. Do you have sawdust or diatomaceous earth? Do you have a gardening section?"

"Yeah. They are fenced off out back. But the gates are open. We got more wood shavings. How much do you need?"

"All of it. Do you have a kitchen?"

Doreen shook her head.

"Then I'll need a barbeque grill and propane tank, glass bowls or beakers, and other cookware. Ice and cold water...."

"What are we making?" Devon asked.

"Mother of Satan."

"Never heard of it."

"Every terrorist on the planet knows about it."

"Why's it called that?"

"Because we will probably kill ourselves, making it."

Devon, Paver, and Doreen leaned back.

Wilcox said, "Let's get to work. Stevie? Where'd you put that cart with the pipes?"

Chapter 7 Overlook

Hard-soled boots clomped across the rooftop. "I told you." Stevie joined Wilcox.

She said, "I wondered where you went after we stopped those things coming in the side door."

"The doors are still locked?" Wilcox looked over from a pair of binoculars.

"Yeah." Stevie nodded.

"They're asleep." Wilcox peered through the binoculars again. "They're all gathered into groups under the parking lot lights."

"Asleep standing up?"

"Those three standing by the road were there earlier. Those three people seem to be talking. They're in complete darkness, unlike the others. I'd say they are hiding in open view. They want us to think they're like the others, but their actions and inaction tells me they are different." He handed her the binoculars.

Stevie asked, "Different?"

He said, "Different. Strange. They aren't like the others."

She scanned from swaying, snoring zombies to the group he mentioned. "Do Zombies sleep?"

"There's only one way to find out."

"You're not going out there?"

"I am."

"Cool. Can I go with you?" Her eyes shined. Her mouth gaped.

He grunted approval, and she hugged him. He smelled her hair and remembered Ellie. The two used the same shampoo or soap.

He pushed her to arms-length. She was a kid. He thought sixteen, maybe fifteen. Too young. He was almost nineteen. He loved Ellie. Stevie wasn't going to happen. She wasn't much older than Sammy. "Okay, okay. This all isn't fun. It's not a game. Don't you have any family?"

"Fuck no."

"No mother? No dad? No brothers or sisters?"

She didn't respond.

"No one?"

"I... I..." She cried. Her legs gave out. She slid to her knees.

"Hey, hey, hey." Wilcox put an arm around her to keep her from falling. His hand scooped the small of her back, lowering her to sit on the store's rooftop.

"My mom... My damn step-dad. I hate that place."

"You can..."

"I have to go back." She faltered, wiped her tears, and cleared her voice. "I'm sorry."

"Don't be."

"I... He... I left home. I was on that bus because I'm running away."

"Where are you going?"

"I don't care. I didn't care. Then all this happened." She gasped, gulping for air. "That bastard said it was hard in the real world."

Wilcox gripped her shoulders. "He didn't mean this. All this is temporary."

"I hope not."

"Huh? You hope not?"

Stevie said, "I'm happy now."

Wilcox's mouth fell open. "Why? You said you were scared."

"I want to kill people. For as long as I can remember, I've wanted to kill people. I used to dream about killing everyone."

"Everyone?"

She nodded. "People suck. This is my day! I can off as many people as I want and get away with."

Wilcox chuckled and asked, "Like you're a serial killer?"

"Um... No. An executioner."

"That's why you want to go out there? To kill people?"

Stevie smiled. "I want to get close and learn the best way to kill these monsters. You're a soldier. You know how to kill with a knife. Teach me."

Wilcox shrugged, thinking perhaps having an intern would be fun. "You can watch us make bombs."

"That'll be cool."

Wilcox said, "This will end. What happens in a day or two, when this is all over?"

"I guess I'll go home."

"Why did you leave?"

"You know. I can't remember much after the first time." She paused. "I was raped."

"By your step-father?"

She nodded. Wilcox leaned and whispered, "Give me a name and address. This whole zombie thing might make a good cover for me to cut his balls off and choke him to death on them."

She laughed and then fell silent. Tears formed once more.

He wrapped his arms around her, offering friendship and sympathy. "It's going to be okay. We'll get out of here. Kill a bunch of zombies. Get a car and hit the road. It can't be like this everywhere. In a little while, Madam President will come out and say, 'The disturbances caused by mass hysteria as a result of protesters disrupting the peaceful organizations celebrating World Protest Week have been quelled.'"

Stevie laughed with a cry. "That's not what's going on."

"I know."

"This will never end." She stepped away from him.

"But that's what the government will say... What

exactly is this?"

She shrugged. "I don't know. I don't care. All I want is to go home to my room, close the door, lock it, and go to sleep."

"And...?"

"And if that asshole comes in, I'll cut his balls off and choke him with them."

Wilcox laughed.

The parking lot lights, street lights, and distant beacons of porchlights across the town dimmed, flickered, and faded to darkness as the electric grid failed.

"Now what?" Stevie stood and walked to the edge of the roof. The crowds of zombies remained.

Wilcox stood behind her. "This isn't going to end in a few days."

"No. It's not."

They returned to the roof hatch and climbed into darkness.

Chapter 8 Recycling

Beau caught a ride a mile from the house. He climbed into the passenger side of a pickup truck driven by a middle-aged, clean-shaven man, "Where ya' going?"

"Recycling plant."

"That's not too far. Ya working the late shift?"

"Eleven to seven."

"Graveyard... Makes for lonely nights?"

"Long nights. Not lonely. There's six of us. Sometimes I wish I could work alone."

"I know how you feel. My wife is out of town, visiting relatives. Glad to have some space, but then I get to missing the company."

They fell silent. Two miles passed. The driver put his hand on Beau's thigh as the truck rolled to a stop at an intersection. The man said, "I live right up here. Would you like to come for a cup of coffee before I drop you at work?"

"N...N... No, sir." Beau opened the door as the truck began to roll forward. He hopped out.

The driver stopped short, sending the door swinging wide and snapping it back. "Where are you going?"

"I forgot something at home." Beau stepped fast, moving towards the back of the truck.

"I'll take you home. You'll be late for work."

"It's okay." Beau crossed behind the truck and started down the side street that offered an alternate route to the recycling plant. He tossed sideways glances at the vehicle, looking to see if it followed him.

In the dim interior light, Beau saw the driver look back on both sides, check his mirrors, then lean across the seat and close the passenger door. He proceeded across the intersection and turned into a driveway. The truck backed into the street turned around. It returned to the junction with its directional light on to follow Beau down the side road.

Before the truck could make the turn and cast its headlights on him, Beau stepped over a ditch at the edge of the pavement, pushed into tall weeds and crossed into a hay-field on the other side. He crouched into the grass as the headlights scanned over his head. The truck drove down the street a hundred yards, turned around and came back.

The driver passed by again and turned toward the Wilcox home, but Beau waited five minutes as his adrenaline rushed at that thought that the man wanted to rape him, or worse. He'd heard about people disappearing in the area, a few in the same town over the years. He recalled his dad had warned him about strangers, but Beau knew he was no longer a child. No monsters lingered under beds. But demons often disguised themselves as humans, and this one, this random ride on the way to work–Beau gasped–better to hide in the grass for a few more minutes– better than drugged, raped, getting a shovel to the head, and dumped into a shallow grave in the woods.

The truck returned. Traveling slow, it turned down the side street and went by the hiding spot again. The driver accelerated up the road before stopping fast and turning around. It came back at a higher rate of speed. Beau panicked when it slammed on the brakes at the intersection. His fear grew with the thoughts of having been spotted. The driver rolled the truck through the intersection and departed and didn't return.

Beau sighed at the chase ending with the knowledge that he'd have to watch out for himself along this road. The creepy old man would be back tonight, or someday. He knew the stranger would be furious and dangerous. He had to protect himself or quit the job, and he wasn't going to leave.

***

An hour later, Beau trudged through the steel door to the factory. Under the oppressive din of machinery crunching and rattling day and night, he scanned his fingerprints into the time clock. The red letters, 'Late, 7 minutes,' appeared on the screen. He scowled.

After he removed his jacket, he hung it in a locker along the wall. A pair of ear-muzzles and gloves sat in a cubby-hole with his name on it. He put on the necessary protection and shuffled to the line.

Coworkers congregated for the change of shift. No one complained about his lateness. They'd dock him fifteen minutes of pay and give seven minutes of it to them. The company still profited from the extra work.

The group of men and women spilled meaningless gossip about someone. Not him. He didn't care anyway.

The group broke at the sound of a trash truck beeping on the tipping floor adjacent to the building. The diesel engine of the front-end loader started up as a new container of recyclables was fed into the giant hopper that moved the material onto conveyor belts.

Beau took his spot beyond the giant electro-magnets that picked up ferrous metal waste and dropped it into bins. Another worker in coveralls stood ready to swap containers as they were filled up.

The presort station removed large items such as cardboard, by bouncing it over large rubber disks. The smaller material fell through the line to conveyors below that that led to further sorting machines, grinding away as it separated paper products. Those lines led to the floor, where workers hand-sorted the detritus of cans, small broken toys, and non-magnetic metal, to a series of other conveyors. Paper went into another baling machine. Glass and plastic, much of it broken, separately went into dumpsters to be melted down. Garbage, wood, and unrecognizable detritus went to the landfill.

Beau settled into his daily, reoccurring, and extended daydreams for the first morning-beer, after shift, then sleeping through the morning hours. He longed to sleep at night. Not having to work was better, but no winning lottery ticket appeared.

Half-way through the first spill of the night shouting came from the truck-spill areas where the loader worked.

Recyclables shortly stopped coming down the belt, and with nothing to pick through and sort, Beau looked at Kerry, Tammy, Nancy, and Charlie. They all stood listening to yelling that grew louder and more violent. Then the noise stopped, and after a moment, they all wandered through the open side door to see what the delay might be.

The loader sat empty. Frank lay on the ground

bleeding from multiple cuts on his face arms, and legs. A tear in his coveralls showed his leg had been removed from the knee down. Tendons waved in the man's struggles. Blood flowed from the open wound.

A woman yelled as the group of co-workers ran to the man's rescue.

Beau watched two bloody men wielding hatchets, running into the woods across the lot. One of them carried a hunk of meat with a work boot laced to the end. They disappeared into the trees, consumed by night.

When Charlie called out for them to stop, they turned and glared back in their direction. One raised the ax in a warning. The other man began to eat the leg, and blood covered his face. Teeth pulled and tore at the skin.

Charlie put his hands up, stepped back, and vomited.

As Beau watched, he heard someone calling for a first-aid kit. Someone else was on the phone, repeatedly trying to explain that they needed an ambulance and the police.

Beau's ordinarily cold eyes livened, and he began to smile. He began to laugh until Charlie dragged him to the ground and yelled at him to stop.

Charlie's efforts worked only to lower Beau's volume. He continued to smirk and hiccup in joy until long after the police arrived.

He heard a cop talking. "...have him held for evaluation."

No, Beau thought. They weren't going to put a hand on him.

The officer said, "He's acting weird. No one is that happy at a murder scene."

Beau stopped smiling.

Another officer turned the first one away, and they walked to their patrol car. "Everyone acts differently. Give him a break. Awful enough for a kid to witness."

Beau stopped laughing. He deliberately put on a mask of somber seriousness and grief as he consoled his work-mates. Then he went back inside and waited for the recycling factory to start again. It wouldn't take long. Only money mattered to these people.

Chapter 9 Power Down

"The power is out." Doreen met Wilcox and Stevie with a flashlight at the bottom of the ladder. "The emergency lights will run off batteries for several hours. I've got the teens collecting flashlights and candles. People are bunking down in the furniture and camping sections. Do you need a sleeping bag?"

"I'm not sleeping." Wilcox accepted a flashlight.

"Do you need anything to eat? There's lots of candy, protein bars, and oatmeal." Doreen smiled.

"No. Thank you."

"That's a joke."

"Huh?"

"Oatmeal… made from all the cattle feed we sell."

"I get it."

"Funny. Isn't it?" She insisted.

"Save the grain. If this plan doesn't work, we'll be eating oatmeal for weeks. Get some rest."

"What are you planning?"

"I'll brief everyone in the morning. Right now, I've got more work to do."

"If you don't mind…" She shifted from foot to foot, head down, staring at the floor.

"Go to bed, Doreen. Find somewhere to sleep. Things will seem brighter in the morning." He offered platitudes without sympathy, knowing people would die before this battleground cleared. He needed cooperation, and he hated to admit he'd taken a leadership position. One plan filled his thoughts. He wanted a better one. The one he has he didn't like, but he needed everyone to work together. They needed to be a team. A team needs a leader. The concept of him leading made him ill.

All his past criticisms of bosses, lieutenants, and captains with their heads up their butts, might have been wrong. His skills rarely lacked when he knew he was correct. When he was uncertain, he could admit his doubts. But now? Would these people follow a doubter? No. His dad taught him to be tough and do what's right. He needed to talk, educate, and train the others. With little time he wondered if he could do that? He'd have to tell them what he wanted and hoped they understood. His father could have done it. The man had died too soon to show him more. He was on his own, and he did the best with the skills and knowledge he could gather. He guessed. He pondered. He made plans with the information he had. He followed those plan and held fast the idea that plans often change. He had and always would change direction when he needed to.

He found a chair in Doreen's office and sat at the desk under the glow of the emergency lights shining in from the storeroom. He laughed, wondering if this is what managers do– relax, do nothing, and think. But thinking with a clear head was difficult under the adrenalin and exhaustion clouding his mind.

He knew how to hunt prey animals. He'd been doing that since he was ten. Predators-who-shoot-back might be more difficult. He'd never hunted for mountain lion or bear. The vicious enemy outside had to be as tricky or more-so because, he wanted to believe, deep down these creatures were still human.

The fight at the door had become a numbers game. They won only because too many dead filled the doorway.

Using their numbers against them would fail outside the store. The parking lot hosted hundreds—the town, perhaps thousands. Beyond the horizon, across the country, John wondered if there were hundreds of millions.

Leaving the store would be dangerous, but he to get home. These other people, these followers he and Paver and Devon had attracted, needed to go their ways as well. He could not be responsible for them forever. A few hours, a day. No more.

Devon, Paver, Stevie, and several others looked to him for answers. Perhaps, to the civilians, the uniform put him in charge—him, a private. Too late to turn away from the responsibility, his concern for his own life joined with that of the group, and their survival. He needed to get them out, get them on the road, so they could all go home and begin salvaging their old lives. They needed to protect their loved ones.

The one strategy he had, he didn't like. That thought would go unspoken.

The power returned. The lights flashed and flickered. Cheers echoed across the store as people doused their flashlights.

Chapter 10 Janine

Beau's memory of the night shift grew vague as he walked the five miles home. He found that the loss of details helped him return to the muffled throb of his daily routines. He'd enjoyed the attack for the sake of something different breaking the surface of his dull life. Any single night had become like any other. Working at the plant was meaningless, and someone getting murdered, Beau thought, "That did the guy a favor."

He went to the shed to grab a beer before going into the house.

"Fuck John and his beer." Beau popped open the can, pulled it down, grabbed another one from the fridge, and went to the back door. He pushed the unlocked door open and stepped into the kitchen. No sounds came.

"Auntie?" Beau stopped outside Kimberly's bedroom. She should have been up, getting ready for her morning shift job at the bakery while he cooked. Most days she sipped a cup of coffee with him and ate an egg or two on toast before leaving for the bakery-job. He always washed the dishes.

She replied, "I don't feel good."

Beau pushed the door open a sliver. "Can I get you anything?"

"No. I need to sleep."

"Okay, Auntie."

He went back into the kitchen and gathered a frying pan, some eggs from the refrigerator–the light was out, he'd have to get one from the shed–some milk, a loaf of bread, and coffee.

Beau prepared the coffee and set it to start, turned on the stove, and put a pat of butter into the pan to heat up. Then he scrambled the eggs in a bowl.

Footfalls like horses clomped down the stairs as Danny, Janine, and Sammy rushed into the kitchen.

"We're going to the river," Sammy said.

"You're having breakfast first," Beau replied. "Kim isn't feeling good, and we need to take care of her." He paused and then said, "Maybe playing outside will let her get some rest. We have eats first."

The children turned and went to their seats at the table. Danny took a chair at the end where Johnny sat when he was home. Sammy pushed him off the chair and took his place. The two wrestled until Beau spoke loudly, "Not again. Cut it out."

They fell silent.

Beau turned from the stove, fiddled with the toaster, and then looked at the coffee maker. "Not again." He said more passively. "Sammy? Go to the shed and flip the breakers in the shed. The electricity is out again."

Danny ran to the door and went out, slamming it behind him. Janine followed her other brother, sticking her tongue out at Sammy and mouthing the words, "You have to stay here with big-Beau." Janine then put her arms out from her sides and waddled to the door, mocking her cousin.

"Janine?" Beau said.

She immediately dropped her arms, and her face went pale.

"Get the bacon."

She ran out the door to catch up with her brother.

Sammy laughed as Beau scowled.

***

"He wants the bacon," The little girl said as she caught up to Danny.

"I like bacon." Danny gave a toothy smile as he reached up to the electrical panel and started to flip switches off and on.

"Me too."

"It's pigs you know," Danny said. "It's made from little piggies like the Three-Little-Pigs." He worked his way down the rows turning each breaker off and back on with a click-click, click-click.

"No, it's not." Janine's brow sank as she fretted.

"Yes, it is."

"No, it's not."

"Yup. Like Little Miss Piggie on that cartoon. You eat little piggies that Johnny shoots and butchers."

"No, he doesn't."

"Yes, he does. We do it. It's natural. Pigs are food."

Janine opened the refrigerator and grabbed a paper-wrapped bundle labeled, 'Bacon.' She turned the package over and over in her hands, staring at it. She whispered to herself, "No, it's not. No. It's not. I don't eat piggies."

Danny pushed by her and said, "Yes, you do."

She swung out at him and dropped the package.

She bent, picked it up, and then she saw Danny staring into the field beyond the smokehouse.

"What is it, Danny?"

"People."

"People?" Janine walked over to see.

Several people walked across the tall grass toward the house. They strolled, looking left and right, sniffing the air, swinging their heads, turning as if to listen for something.

Danny said, "There's nothing from that way but the river and the hills. Where are they coming from?"

"What?"

"Why would anyone come from over there? The road is that way." Danny half-turned and threw an arm to indicate the long driveway.

As they stood watching, three people in the front stopped, turned in complete circles, and then faced the house again. They crouched, hands, and elbows touching the ground. They hung their heads between their knees and then they jumped into the air and came towards the siblings at a leaping-gorilla gait. The people behind them started to run.

"Go inside. We have to go inside. Run. Run." Danny ran for the house. "Mom! Beau! Sammy! Get the guns."

Janine dropped the bacon and stood to watch the mass of people coming at her. She heard her brother hollering something, but he was always yelling anyway. As she looked around, she couldn't find him. He was gone. She turned for the shed and ran through the double doors. She looked for Danny inside as she pulled one of the doors closed. As she reached over her head for the metal handle and pulled the second door closed, several filthy, blood covered hands wrapped around the door and pulled it open.

The little girl screamed as the creatures sniffed the air and searched with cloudy-white eyes.

"Janine! Janine!" She heard Danny call from the porch as she watched the strange creatures open the shed doors.

"Janine!"

The porch door slammed.

"Janine!"

A firearm banged.

"Get the bacon."

One of the creatures struck the workbench with an ax handle.

"Janine!"

The shed doors banged open.

"Get the bacon."

She screamed, ran, and hated her cousin. She'd always hated her cousin.

Chapter 11 The Plan

Wilcox retrieved his cell phone. He listened to the phone ring. No one answered. He hung up and dialed again.

"Johnny? Johnny?" Kimberly's voice waned faint and weak on the noisy connection.

"Mom? Are you okay?"

"I'm fine. Did you hear the news?"

"Yes. I heard it on the radio." He lied, not wanting her to know he'd fought through the middle of the nightmare.

She asked, "Are you okay?"

"I'm good. How is everyone there?"

"Where are you?"

"In Branson."

"You didn't make it to…"

"Not yet… Paver and Devon are with me. The bus broke down. There was an accident."

"An accident!?"

Wilcox reprimanded himself for saying that. "It's all right. No one was hurt." More lies. "Mom… I'm…"

"What is it?"

"I'm coming home."

"You need to report for duty."

"I'm worried about you… Mom? This…" He didn't want to relay the horrors he'd seen. He didn't want to recall them himself. Whatever she saw on the news was enough, and the reports would downplay the attacks as disturbances and riots to alleviate fears of what it was: mass insanity, mass murder brought on by something. What? A disease? A virus? Poison in the water supply? He didn't know. The government, the army too, wanted order and compliance and security. They'd tell the news what to report. He sighed. "I'm coming home."

"You'll get in trouble."

Wilcox struggled with the idea of honesty and decided to remain silent. It could wait. He worried that she relied on his paycheck to fill the gaps in the household expenses. He risked arrest and reduction in rank, pay, court-martial, and a dishonorable discharge if he didn't get to Fort Leonard Wood within. How long? He thought, a day at most.

"You don't worry, ma." He brightened his voice.

"As long as you are okay. You need to…"

"We'll hitchhike. We'll get there. Do you have lights? Food?"

"Promise me you are going to Missouri."

"Mom…?"

"We have what we need. The power's gone out before. It'll be back on in a day or two. Danny worked the smokehouse and made some jerky and salted meats from the deer."

"Tell him to stay indoors."

"Oh, Johnny. Everything is okay."

"Mom. Tell the kids to stay inside, and you stay home. Don't be going to work, call in sick, and keep your gun loaded."

"You worry too much."

"I learned it from you. I need you to ask Beau something. Tell him he needs to board up the house."

"That's silly."

"There's enough plywood from the old chicken coop and two-by-fours in the shed. Tell Beau to block all the first-floor windows."

"There's no…"

"The riots are everywhere. People have gone insane."

"We're out in the country. Please stop worrying…"

"Mom…?" Wilcox heard the fear in his mother's voice while she tried to assay him of his worries. She knew. He hated himself for putting such stress on her, but she might already know. He had to say it for himself. To help accept the horror. But did she know the full extent? Could he tell over the phone?

"Johnny, I wanted to…" The call dropped.

Wilcox tried to call again and received dead air. He called several more times without success. What, he thought, did she want to say? What did she need? Was it something for him or someone else to do? What? Report in? Screw general orders. Screw new orders. Fort Leonard Wood is gone. Going home would be next, or now. Right now.

He said to himself, "I need to leave." With a raised

voice, he called out. "Meeting. Everyone to furniture. We need to talk."

Ten minutes later, after word spread and people gathered, many having stopped to take snacks from the food aisle, the meeting started.

Cart-Woman rolled up in a new cart. She only stood when the batteries died, and that was just long enough to switch to new wheels. Paver and Devon stood beside Wilcox. Stevie stayed back, leaning against shelves. Gerald and April took camouflage-pattern lounge chairs, and Tim and Barry shared a camouflage couch. The store was consistent.

Wilcox nodded to them and asked, "Where's Chuck?"

His audience cast glances around the room. Someone asked, "Who?"

"The big-chested guy," Wilcox replied and then shrugged.

Doreen, two teenaged girl cashiers that Wilcox didn't recall seeing before, and the stock boys pulled garden benches off bottom shelves to sit on. Tank-Top Kid lay on a queen-sized mattress, covered with a camouflage quilt, a few feet away.

Wilcox coughed and said, "We can't stay here."

"What's the plan? Army-man." Tank-Top Kid laughed.

Wilcox said, "The zombies aren't active at night. We all need to go. None of us can stay here."

"Why not?" Tim asked.

"They will get inside. There's a thousand in the parking lot, surrounding the building. They seem to sleep standing up at night. In the darkness they don't hunt, they don't fight. They only attack during the day."

"What if we want to stay?" Cart-Woman flippantly asked. She stuffed a candy bar into her mouth.

Wilcox wondered how the obese woman might escape if she wanted to. "We all have families out there, somewhere."

She took another bite and spoke as she chewed. "We have food, water. We can last weeks."

"Not if the zombies get in."

Paver and Devon echoed his words.

Barry said, "What do you mean they don't attack at night? How do you know?"

"We watched them from the rooftop. I think... I think they have night-blindness. Did you see their gray eyes? And..."

"I don't want to leave." Cart-Woman grew grave. Her sarcasm passed. "You can't make us go."

Devon said, "Who will stay and protect you?"

"You will."

Paver laughed. "I'm going home."

"You're soldiers. You need to protect us."

"We will," Wilcox said. "Long enough to get to a car and drive out of here."

Cart-woman said, "You need to stay here. Wait for the police. Call in reinforcements. Isn't that what it's called? Reinforcements? The cavalry?"

"The police are gone. The Army is gone. There's no one left."

Doreen spoke. "It's true. Biblical end-times. It's my store. I'm responsible for what's here, but what's here is all there is and all there'll be. If this thing ends someday, it won't be for days or weeks. I can't hope for that. I have a husband. I hope he's at home and I pray he's safe. I'm leaving."

"Who's going out and who's staying?"

A cacophony of arguments rose.

Wilcox banged the handle of his knife on a metal shelf.

When the group fell quiet, he said, "I need to know."

Cart-Woman said, "We get to vote. We have a democracy. We get to elect what we do. We all stay, or we all leave."

"This isn't a democracy. Each decides on his or her own."

Cart-woman raised her voice. "If you open the doors to get out, the zombies will get in."

"Then close the doors behind us. Who goes?"

Stevie stepped forward. Gerald, Doreen, and the teenagers raised their hands.

"April?"

She shook her head.

"You others?"

The small group of other shoppers frowned, bit lips, shook their heads side-to-side, and fretted.

Cart-Woman smiled.

"You on the bed?" Wilcox raised his head.

Tank-Top Kid said, "I'm going out."

Tim said, "I'm with her. We'll protect the store."

Cart-Woman's smile faded. "You leave the guns."

Wilcox ignored her. "Whoever has a gun keeps it. Who's got car-keys?"

"Whoever has a car, keeps it." Cart-Woman snickered under the jiggle of keys pulled from her pocket.

"What's the plan?" Gerald asked.

Wilcox replied, "You were good in that fight. What's your background?"

"Marines."

"I'll forgive you." Wilcox laughed.

"Don't worry. I won't leave you Army guys behind. One Marine–One Battle."

Wilcox grew serious and said, "Here's my idea…"

***

Wilcox assembled components and constructed explosives from the ammo reloading supplies. He had Stevie help him as they unrolled Gorilla Tape and stuck match-after-match together to make twenty and thirty-foot fuses. They drilled holes in pipe-end-caps and fed fuses through the opening. They greased the threads on the ends of stud-pipes, screwed a cap on, filled the pipes with gunpowder and black powder, and sealed the end. The grease kept the threads from sparking or getting too hot, and Wilcox was careful to not-overtighten the ends. The threads gave grip to seal, not the force used to lock it down.

He asked for help from everyone who happened by, and he inspected and confirmed the work they did. He asked the stock boys for fireworks.

Doreen said, "No," but the boys left and came back with armloads of roman-candles and sparklers as well as 'artillery tubes' and shells. They carried cherry bombs, smoke bombs, snaps, and firecrackers.

Wilcox said, "Nice job! Where'd you…"

"Doreen doesn't know, but we hid these after the Fourth of July. Meant to set them off in the parking lot."

"Well, you're gonna get a chance to. Get some poster paper and cut-open or unroll all of it. We need the power inside."

Doreen and Paver brought cast-iron cooking pots. Wilcox drilled row after row of divots, not quite all the way through, into the thick iron. He said to Stevie, "This weakens the metal in a pattern, so the pot breaks into shrapnel." He drilled six holes around the lid, aligned to six more holes in the pot where he explained he would bolt the covers down. "I wish you had a pressure cooker."

Stevie left and returned ten minutes later, not with pressure-cookers, but carrying a hundred-foot roll of fuse-cord.

"You're a doll!" Wilcox exclaimed, and she blushed. "Any dynamite? Detonator caps?"

She shook her head.

Wilcox filled the pots with gunpowder and nails. He said, "The nails do extra damage."

***

When they had finished, they had six pipe-bombs and four pot-bombs. They each hoped it would be enough.

Wilcox said, "We'll use these to clear a path through the zombies. That should give us a running start to get to the cars and get the hell out of here."

Devon said, "We'll need to draw them in for the bombs to be most effective. But drawing them in will bring more of them at a run."

"We have to time it right."

"Throw the pipebombs like grenades and light the fuses on the cook-pot? Wait. Then run-n-gun?"

"And pray."

Devon laughed. "I've been praying inside since this whole thing started. My momma'll be praying too."

Wilcox stowed pipe bombs in his cargo pockets. He handed two to Devon and two more to Paver. He asked, "Did you talk to her?"

Devon said, "Yeah. It seems the white-ass zombies stay on their side of the tracks. They don't like us either. Damn racists."

Paver asked, "She's okay? Your mom? Is she all right?"

Devon replied, "Talked to her on the phone. Praying and using a fry-pan to bash anyone trying the front door. I asked her if they were zombies or emergency responders. She said it didn't matter who they were. Just get off her porch, or Thom was gonna get the shotgun."

Wilcox asked, "Does Thom have a shotgun?"

"Sure does. But Momma's frying pan saves ammo. She said she'd killed three and they are starting to stink up the porch."

Wilcox said, "Let's get home to help them. Tonight we sneak out and set these suckers under cars, right under the fuel tanks, and run the fuses under the front doors. When they go off, they'll send shrapnel sideways, take out their legs, and hopefully, the gas tanks blow or burn."

"No trip-wires?" Paver asked.

"This is gonna be a hell-dance. We can't have one of those wandering things starting the music too early."

The three friends crept outside long after the skies grew dark and placed the bombs and ran the fuses.

Chapter 12 Escape

On the rooftop, as the false dawn rose, Wilcox pointed to the three placid zombies who'd spent the entire time standing, facing each other. "Kill those three."

"Okay." Tank-Top gave a crooked, dirty-toothed grin.

"You aren't going to ask me why?"

"Because you said so."

"Man. I like you." Wilcox laughed. "I think those three zombies control all the other zombies. If you kill them, the rest won't know where to go or who to attack. There might be other leaders, but don't miss them!"

"I won't."

Wilcox said, "There are only three rounds for that rifle."

"Three dead zombie-masters. What if there's more of them?"

Wilcox was uncertain what to call those who seemed to control and direct the others, but he knew what the boy meant. He said, "We can't know. We can only try to get people out and save our necks too. How will you get out?"

Tank-Top said, "When you open the doors, the bombs go off, and all hell comes around the front. I'll go down the ladder and out the back. There are woods out back, and I'm good in the woods."

Wilcox shook the young hillbilly's hand. "Good plan. Good luck."

Wilcox knew he should ask for the man's name and stop thinking of him by the clothes he wore, but if the boy died, he didn't want to know how, and if he died in agony, he didn't want to know his name. It'd be easier to forget him among the thousands who'd already perished. He granted himself that one concession, that one lapse in his manners and personal values. He knew he needed to protect his emotional state as much as his own life and the lives of others.

"Us rednecks need all the luck we can get."

"Give me three minutes before you shoot. As soon as I hear you shoot, I'll light the fuses. Then it's all hell and earth and fire and damnation."

Tank-Top Kid, "This is fun."

Wilcox descended the ladder.

***

Three minutes later, as Wilcox held a cigarette lighter in his hand, he heard the shots. He hoped the bullets flew true and the zombie-masters were dead.

Flicking the wheel, he produced a flame and held it to the bundle of fuses that ran under the roll-up doors. The previous night, he and Devon snuck out and planted the pot-bombs. Some near the entrance and others further out, under gas tanks of cars. They'd slowly and quietly moved between and through groups of zombies that stood sleeping.

The homemade match-tip fuses burned fast and furious. The fuse-cord burned a bit slower.

"Wait for it! Ears. Cover your ears!" He yelled to Devon and Paver, who stood ready to open the roll-up doors, and they all put hands or forearms up to protect their hearing.

The gunshots brought activity from the zombies. The monsters ran back and forth over the fuses as evidenced by their footfalls. Then they banged on the doors.

An eternal ten seconds passed before the bombs exploded. The floors and walls shook. The plop and splatter of blood and formerly-internal organs came from all directions.

"Now," Wilcox called.

Gerald steadied his rifle between shots, taking careful aim, while Devon and Paver ran the door up. Zombies approached the rattling steel door while the soldiers retrieved the pipe bombs from cargo pockets.

The zombies approached. They stumbled over the injured-but-not-killed creatures caught in the initial blasts. The wounded thrashed broken legs and arms on the ground.

Clawed-hands on ears bled purple. By turning their heads as if disoriented, deafened, and startled by the explosions, the monsters found the door.

The men lit the fuses on the pipe-bombs and tossed them out the doors. As they threw the grenades, a teenage employee ran screaming through the front door wielding an ax.

Wilcox yelled, "No."

The grenades exploded, throwing nails and bolts. The shrapnel ripped through the boy, tossing him back. He landed in a heap at Wilcox's feet. The body leaked no blood, and no broken bones were apparent. The boy lay unmoving, unresponsive, every bit dead.

"What the fuck?" Paver yelled, looking from the boy's body to Wilcox, and scanning the approaching zombies.

Devon grabbed Wilcox, "We've got to get out of here."

Cart-Woman cackled as she pointed to zombies and then to his men and the others in the store.

"She's one of them," Wilcox said.

"What?" Devon hollered.

"She's a zombie." Wilcox drew his knife and started towards Cart-Woman.

She backed away with her feet for the battery in the cart had died, but Devon grabbed him. The big man yelled over the grunting and growls that grew as the enemy came.

Devon yelled, "We leave now. We have to go."

"She's one of them." Wilcox pulled out of his grip.

The woman didn't deny it. Her round pasty white face showed no fear. She stopped retreating and resumed directing zombies into the store.

Devon said again, "We have to go."

Wilcox looked out the door as a dozen zombies entered. Beyond them, hundreds more turned and approached.

Wilcox led the way through the mass, sticking his knife into their heads, pulling it free, and moving to the next one.

Devon and Paver followed, firing the last of their ammo, and drawing knives and hammers to kill as they went. Gerald came next, discharging his rifle until it went dry and then using it as a club.

Stevie, Doreen, and four of the teenagers came out carrying hand-weapons, engaging zombies that tried to encircle the soldiers.

"Break out," Wilcox called over his shoulder. "Run. Don't fight."

One of the boys headed for a car.

Two girls followed Doreen. Three zombies tackled

one. Her last words were lost in a stifled yelp as she disappeared into a fountain of blood and body parts.

As Wilcox cleared the first wave, he looked back at Cart-Woman. She continued directing zombies inside the store. The plan of those to stay behind and close the doors failed. Cart-Woman, as the leader of that group, smiled and laughed for her deception was complete, and her rabid and insanity driven slaves feasted on human flesh.

"I want her dead," Wilcox yelled.

"Another time," Devon answered.

They moved through the parking lot, looking for a car that Stevie had pointed out next to the body of a man. Wilcox spied the keys on the ground where she had seen from the rooftop. He blessed her sharp eyes as he scooped them up and unlocked the doors. The four men climbed in.

As Wilcox drove away, he saw Stevie's long hair and head tilted forward over the wheel of a car. She scanned the parking lot looking for zombies to run over and avoiding parked cars and light poles. She turned away as she drove north out of the parking lot.

"She'll be okay," he said.

Paver asked from the back seat, "Who?"

As they left Branson behind, Wilcox's memory failed as he struggled to recall seeing what had happened to the others and where they had gone during the battle. His adrenaline slowed. His heart rate normalized, but still, he couldn't recall. He prayed those who dashed the parking lot would be safe, and he said, "There's always hope." He silently regretted that, because those who stayed inside the store, where screams and death reigned, certainly had none. He shook his head for in his mind he heard Cart-Woman's cackling laughter. It was a sound that would inescapably follow him.

Chapter 13 Pawnshop

Wilcox drove south on Highway 65 to Arkansas. He jammed on the brakes and turned the wheel hard as his companions hollered.

"Ammo," Wilcox said as the car skidded in the dirt in front a pawn-shop. The building appeared closed up. No lights burned inside or out, the grated and barred windows and doors were dark through the dust and grime.

Gerald said, "Looks deserted. Could be ten years or more."

"No broken glass. We're going in." Wilcox got out of the car and walked to the door. It was locked. He kicked it four times before the door frame gave way.

The other men gathered around him.

Paver grinned and called inside, "We're home. Anyone here?"

No answer.

Wilcox put his hand where his handgun should be and found the holster empty. He vaguely recalled dropping it during the gun battle after it ran dry. He raised his hands instead and called into the store. "Hello? Don't shoot. We want to talk and trade."

No sound came from inside.

The light through the windows showed that half of the shelves were empty. Items knocked from shelves littered the floors.

Wilcox said, "Ransacked by the owner? The front door was locked. The back door is probably locked too."

Anything of immediate or high value was gone, and anything not readily usable was left behind. A gun rack behind the glass counters was empty but several boxes of ammunition, along with some few boxes of shotgun shells, lay scattered on the countertops and floor.

The men poured inside. Ammunition rolled free as their boots shuffled and kicked at the debris.

Wilcox said, "Gather the ammo. Take any knives, axes, hammers, and baseball bats."

Devon said, "I want a hockey stick."

Wilcox laughed. "We leave in five minutes." He saw the handle of a Glock protruding from under a wire-mesh shelf. He grabbed the weapon, dropped the magazine, found it loaded, unloaded the ammo from the magazine onto the counter to count the rounds, and then he reloaded the gun. He racked cartridge into the chamber.

He asked, "What'd you guys find."

Devon said, "Some .203 for Paver and me. Not much."

Gerald replied, "I found a few rounds of 30-06."

Wilcox looked around. "Anything else?"

They waited for a moment, walked through the store and back to look it over one more time, and then Wilcox said, "Let's go home."

Chapter 14 MRAP-Badger

The voice of a female reporter spoke over a static-filled telephone connection on the car's radio.

"Megan. Little Rock Convention Hall has beds for people with nowhere to go despite the government ending the state of emergency. Calls to government agencies such as Homeland Security, Health and Human Services, and the Center for Disease Control are unanswered."

Megan asked, "Ms. Vasquez. One more question. Can we consider that we are getting conflicting information about the riots?"

"The last Emergency Broadcast message indicated that they are under control."

"Are we in a clean-up phase? What exactly is going

on? Why are shelters being set up?"

Vasquez said, "These facilities are for people with nowhere else to go. There are fires and terrible destruction."

"What are we looking at?"

"FEMA is being proactive and providing facilities for care."

Megan's voice quaked with worry. "Are you saying hospitals are overwhelmed?"

"No. No. The mayor stated that everyone should shelter in place, call 911 but expect delayed police and medical response. If you need immediate medical assistance, ask someone to drive you to the nearest hospital, or go to the convention center. Police, fire, and EMT services are working with limited available resources."

"Geniuses." Paver's sarcastic comment came from the back seat.

Gerald added, "The police can't do squat."

Wilcox and Devon grunted agreement and then remained stoically and knowingly quiet.

The sparse rural traffic increased as they approached the city. People from the county drove inward. Luggage and coolers filled the back seats, hatchbacks, and truck beds as if a mass vacation was in progress. Shotgun racks in pickup trucks held weapons. No doubt existed as to their state of readiness for combat.

Urbanites from Little Rock drove the other direction, escaping into the country-side. A church bus with Korean writing on the side and dozens of people inside traveled north.

A broken-down car on the side of the road had a flat tire. Further up the road, a pickup with its hood up billowed steam. After the truck, three cars had collided.

"Should we help those people?" Wilcox asked.

No one answered. Wilcox continued to pass stranded motorists, one after another, and he suppressed feelings of guilt. He knew what each of his friends thought, and probably too, those people on the road knew, everyone needed to get home to their families. Everyone wanted safety. He felt the same way for he knew his mom and siblings needed him, but then guilt rose for the suggestion which itself was a detriment. It broke their focus and might have weakened the group. His team worked as one. When one wanted to offer aid, they should all help, or at least agree to assist.

Gunfire rose from a group of cars stopped in the median. Wilcox stepped on the gas as they raced onward, putting thoughts of helping others aside. They needed to help their own families.

Twenty minutes later, traffic slowed to a stop. Two camouflage Humvees bearing National Guard logos and a white United Nations MRAP 6x6 blocked the north and south-bound lanes. Cars stopped in front of them, and temporary barriers prevented going around. Southbound vehicles made slow U-turns across the grass and returned north at the orders of soldiers who waved them along with white gloves and sweeping carbine muzzles. A long line of north-bound cars stood idling, waiting. Two guardsmen directed the drivers to turn around with threatening gestures of carbines and rifles. Several other soldiers gathered around the UN armored transport talking, laughing, relaxed, and perhaps bored.

Paver asked, "Is that MRAP a Cougar or a Badger? Mine-Resistant-Ambush-Protected."

Devon said, "Cougars are Marine Corp. That's UN, and these guys are National Guard."

Gerald slid open the chamber of his deer rifle, peered inside, and closed the bolt again. "How can you tell?"

"The dopey looks on their faces." Wilcox stopped, opened his door, and stepped out. His hand went to his belt knife. He pulled it loose, tilted the hilt forward, pushed it down, and felt the scabbard's leather grip the blade.

"Hey. I'm supposed to be the funny one." Paver counted three cartridges as he pushed them into his last magazine. He slapped it back into his AR, cycled the bolt, and followed behind Wilcox. He lowered the muzzle. The gun hung from the shoulder strap but where it would be quick to bear.

"When are you ever funny?" Devon took up the rear behind Gerald as they all walked between the cars towards the blockade. People in vehicles watched them with wide eyes, fearful expressions, and white knuckles on the steering wheels. Individually, they relayed the same fright that gripped everyone and every situation the group had witnessed for several days.

A tall, lean sergeant with a cauliflower ear put on a helmet over high-and-tight blonde hair. He hoisted an M4, muzzle pointing at the sky. "Dogfaces." He gestured to his men and then to Wilcox's team.

Wilcox looked down for an instant, seeing how they must appear: Army fatigues covered in blood and filth.

"Ground pounders," Wilcox said loud enough for them to hear.

"What's your orders?" A blue-helmeted captain, speaking with a thick East London accent, called from the machine gun turret.

The National Guard sergeant put a hand to stop them. "Ya went AWOL?"

Devon scoffed.

Wilcox read the non-com's name tag. "Sergeant Kessel, sir. Our bus got attacked." Wilcox stepped to the side and looked up at the UN officer above. "Captain? Can

I ask what you are doing here?"

"I'll ask the questions." Kessel blocked him. "Let's see ya DA-31."

Paver rubbed his ear with his middle finger and said, "I'll give you a DA-31."

Kessel pointed at Paver, tipped his head, and eyeballed the man as he said to Wilcox, "Where y'all heading?"

"Leonard Wood."

"That's the other direction."

"Detour."

"Zombies?"

"Yeah."

"Good thing ya found us. We'll get ya to Leonard Wood."

The captain rubbed his clean-shaven sunken chin. "Fort Leonard Wood is in Missouri. We're assigned to Arkansas."

"That's enough out of y'll." Kessel turned his head to the senior officer.

Wilcox knew who was in charge and who played soldier. The disrespect of the play soldier concerned him. Despite a UN military officer on American soil, and disregarding posse-comitatus¬–the illegality of soldiers acting in police duties–if the higher-ups give an order, then that's the chain of command. Kessel was talking with insubordination to a senior officer. Wilcox worried. "I lied. We're not going to Leonard Wood."

"Disobeying orders?"

"Orders were canceled."

"Emergency orders from the president say all military and ex-military to report to the nearest fort or armory until new orders issued. Failing that, to fall in with the first unit you find. That's us."

Wilcox noted Kessel didn't mention the peace-keeper.

"We have families. We're going home."

"Deserters? I can arrest you." Kessel continued as the guardsmen stepped forward with weapons at high-ready, leaving the cars to stop or slowly navigate between the barriers. "You're joining us until we can get you back to your unit, or the Governor says otherwise. We need more men and weapons, and you've come at the right time."

Cars stopped in the southbound lanes. North-bound vehicles piled up. Fewer of them made the U-turn without the direction of the soldiers to guide them. People got out to see about the delay, and someone repeatedly blew a horn.

Wilcox recognized the dissolving situational control. He asked, "What's your orders?"

"Secure this road. No one goes into Little Rock, and no one gets out."

"Why?"

"Containment."

"We're not going to Little Rock. We're going around."

"This is the only road, and it's closed. You need to fall in. I'll do a weapons inspection. You're out of uniform. How much ammo you got?" Kessel scanned their weapons.

The captain appeared at his side. "You going home?"

Devon nodded. Paver shrugged. Wilcox said, "Yes, sir."

The officer turned to Kessel. "Let them pass."

"You ain't in charge. You're on joint maneuvers. A damn spectator to how American's do shit."

"The President declared Title 10."

Kessel turned his head to the captain. "What's that?"

"The National Guard is under Presidential control."

"You have no authority here."

"I'm the highest ranking officer present, and that makes me a Unified Commander."

"Unified what?"

Wilcox clarified, "He's in charge."

"You shut up." Kessel turned to Wilcox.

Wilcox fingered the hilt of his knife.

The captain said, "Go back to your car. Sergeant, clear these civilian vehicles. Get them turned around. These men are clear to pass through Little Rock."

"They ain't going anywhere."

"That's an order. Let 'em go." The officer looked at Wilcox and smiled.

"They ain't going anywhere." The sergeant's voice lowered. His eyelids narrowed. He drew a Sig Sauer P320 from a belt holster.

The handgun rose. The muzzle turned as the Captain stepped back. The officer's hands rose to ward off the weapon.

Wilcox's fingers wrapped around the hilt of his knife. The blade cleared the scabbard. He leaned forward into a lunging step.

A shot rang as Kessel released a bullet into the officer's ear. The United Nations captain crumpled as his helmet flew off. Brains splattered the soldiers standing nearby.

Kessel turned the handgun as Wilcox's knife plunged into the sergeant's throat. A gurgling spray of blood spewed from the wound. Kessel swayed on his feet, listing forward against the hilt. Another shot from the handgun went wild.

Silence followed.

Wilcox stood, holding the man on his feet with the knife.

The wide eyes of every soldier and civilian moved from man to man. Each witness struggled to comprehend what had happened. Feet shuffled as nervous energy went undirected. Each man looked into the eyes of each foe.

Each man waited, judged, and pondered what he should do.

As if time slowed and then abruptly increased to faster-than-normal speed, carbines and rifles came to bear. Bolts slammed home. Safeties clicked off. Gun barrels rose, and sights aligned.

Silence came again. A full second passed where no one spoke, no one breathed, no bird chirps, cars on the road stopped, as if time stopped. As if the world ceased to turn. The universe waited.

And then gunfire roared again.

Wilcox pulled his blade from Kessel's throat, dropping the man to the ground. He spun, driving the point into a soldier immediately behind the sergeant.

Gerald shot one of the guardsmen with his deer rifle.

Devon fired, taking down two with his AR. Paver put his last three rounds into a guardsman charging towards him with a bayonet.

The gunfire stopped.

Silence returned.

Seconds passed, and then a slow rolling, rising, chorus of screams came from the civilians. In a chaotic scramble, the drivers and passengers of the cars, and the arena of spectators ran for the woods. Several cars jumped forward, crashed into other vehicles, drove their bumpers into fenders, ripped steel open, turned wheels, and raced across the median and down the highway.

Blood soaked into Wilcox's fatigues as he calmly cleaned his blade on his trousers. He sheathed the weapon, and he scanned for more soldiers, stragglers who might have hidden among the military vehicles. Then he gazed at his men. They stood placid, stoic, not showing the expressions of shock he'd came to expect from everyone. He'd witnessed too much of that these recent days. After killing hundreds of zombies, perhaps violence no longer felt wrong or abnormal.

Wilcox saw Paver.

A guardsman lay dead at his friend's feet, but blood covered the bayonet affixed to the carbine. Paver hugged his empty weapon, snorting quick and shallow through his nostrels. He smiled with tight lips as blood leaked from the corners of his mouth. At a cough, his mouth opened and blood gushed out. He tried to talk, but red bubbling foam came out, and a swishing sound escaped from a hole in his chest. Worry filled his eyes and his legs buckled.

Wilcox stepped to catch his friend as he fell, turn him, and assist him to the pavement. The full weight of the man came on Wilcox. Devon helped as Wilcox's grip slipped, and they placed Paver on the asphalt, landing hard, and banging his head.

Wilcox drew his knife and sliced open Paver's shirt. He yelled, "Get me a med-kit from the MRAP." He pressed the palm of his hand to the bayonet wound. "Don't die. Don't die. Paver? You are okay."

Paver stared into the sky.

"Shit. Shit. Shit." Gerald walked in circles.

Devon knelt to press a finger to Paver's neck and listen to his mouth and nose. He shook his head. "He died standing up... On his feet."

"Fuck me. Fuck this." Wilcox removed his hand. No more blood came. Paver's heart had stopped.

Wilcox stood, stepped to the guardsman who killed Paver and stomped on the dead man's neck. He went to Kessel's body and kicked it a dozen times, repeatedly yelling, "Fuck you. You idiot. You fucking moron. You killed him. You killed your men. You killed everyone."

Each man gave the other room, moving away from each other. Tears, low gasps, and grief filled the space between them.

Chapter 15 Parting Friends

"We need to take the MRAP." Devon frowned as he climbed into the gun turret. "There's another ammo box for the .30 caliber."

"Too slow. I'm twenty miles from home," Wilcox said.

Devon said, "I'm another fifteen miles to the South East, but you're heading South and West."

Wilcox replied, "If we have any hope of helping our families, we need to split up."

"What makes you think things are safer in the city?" Devon pointed from the top of the MRAP. "This will get us anywhere we want to go."

Wilcox said, "We split up and go around the city."

Devon insisted. "We're better together. We're a team."

"No." He pointed to the dead soldiers. "If we go together then the police, the military, everyone will think we are a gang or a band of violent looters. Those cars are driving back into Little Rock..." He waved his arm as the chaos of traffic rose again around them. People gawked at the bloody scene. "They are going to tell the next soldier or cop they meet what happened here. If we split up, we can blend in, bypass these roadblocks, and get home. No more killing people. There are enough zombies for killing." Wilcox retrieved a handgun from the ground near where the sergeant bled out. The red pool mixed with the lieutenant's blood and splattered gray-matter to form a large, creeping puddle in the middle of the road. He took two extra magazines from a belt pouch after he kicked the body to roll it face-up.

Gerald traded his bolt action for an M4. "There's enough cars." He swung the muzzle at the abandoned vehicles on the highway. "But those people... They'll be coming back, and they'll want to know what happened here."

"What do we do about Paver?" Wilcox walked to his fallen friend.

"Does he got family?" Devon climbed out the back of the MRAP.

"Yeah, but where?"

"Don't know. I met Pavilions at a gas station in Pine Bluff."

"He might have a driver's license on him."

"You thinking of driving him home?"

Wilcox paused for a moment and shook his head. "Do we bury him here? There's gotta be a trenching shovel or two. We can't leave him."

Gerald said, "Let's wrap him in blankets and bind it with rope or cord. That'll keep the buzzards off. He'll get a military funeral after this is all over."

Gerald, Devon, and Wilcox collect blankets and towels from various abandoned cars. A pickup truck with camping gear in the back provided a length of rope. They found Paver's military ID in a blood-soaked pocket before binding the body in tightly wrapped cloth and carrying it into the back of the MRAP.

Wilcox said, "Someone should say something."

"I can't say anything…" Devon sniffed and coughed, holding back tears.

Devon shook his head, fighting back his tears.

Wilcox bowed his head as they crouched around the body in the back of the vehicle. "Lord. This man was named Kristian Pavilions by his parents. We call him Paver. He's our friend. Take him home and treat him right. He's a good man, and he deserves better than this crappy world gave him, and if you don't, I'm going to kick your ass when I see you. Amen."

"Why are you dissing God?" Devon said.

"Say, 'Amen,' dammit," Wilcox warned.

"Amen."

Gerald exited the back without a word. They closed the doors behind them, sealing Paver in.

Sounds of moving brush and the cracking of sticks rose from the woods.

"Zombies?" Devon asked.

Wilcox put out a hand. "Probably people coming back for their cars. We need to go."

"Man... We should stick together."

"The best chance your girl and brother have is with you there. We've been gone too long as it is. You're a soldier. Buck up."

"You suck." Devon slapped the hand away and put his arms around Wilcox in a bear-hug. He laughed, short, respectfully. Just as quickly, he pushed off. "Get the hell out of here."

"Yeah." Wilcox smiled. Worried. "Who needs you, anyway?"

"Not you. Can't hit the side of a barn with a hammer."

"You fags." Gerald slung his newly acquired carbine, bumped fists with the others, and strutted off looking inside cars for keys. He found a Charger, climbed in, and with a squeal of the tires, he drove away.

"Well?" Wilcox frowned.

Devon punched Wilcox in the shoulder. "What the fuck you still doing here?"

Wilcox said, "Leaving."

"Smell ya later."

"Are you taking the MRAP?"

"Nah. I wanna operate the .30 cal. but you can't drive for shit. So I'm taking a Humvee and a passel of grenades."

"A passel?" Wilcox laughed.

Devon said, "Yeah. A passel. It means a lot."

"I know what it means. I think that Gerald is right."

The taller soldier said, "Say it."

"You just might be a fag."

"I'm gonna hit you again. Not gentle like before." Devon stepped forward, fists clenched.

Wilcox put his hands out and up. "Take care of yourself. When this is over, whenever that is, I'll catch up with you."

Devon laughed. "Quit being so optimistic. This all is the end of the world. It's never going to stop. Damn Revelations as my momma said. Like in the Bible. We'll never see each other again."

"You believe that?"

"You don't?"

"We'll see each other again." Wilcox sighed.

Devon shook his head. "Take that other Humvee and get the hell outta here before I learn ya what is and isn't."

Chapter 16 Ellie Keating

Wilcox turned onto Whitwell Street and slowed the Humvee as he rolled up to the Keating's house.

The front door was closed, as were the garage doors, and the side screened door.

He turned into the driveway and stopped behind a green sedan. He couldn't remember if they had one car or two. He recalled Ellie having to borrow the car on occasion.

No one exited the house.

He knocked on the front door. The sound of a chair scrapping on a wood floor came from inside.

Someone was there. But who?

He knocked again.

A door closed, softly, as if someone hid inside, pretending the house was unoccupied.

Why aren't they answering the door?

He pressed the doorbell button. No Ring. No electricity.

Did they have a dog? Would they have left it alone? Abandoned? Ellie would never allow that. Could there be zombies inside? His hand went to his holstered handgun, and he stepped back. He glanced right and left at the sides of the house. He looked behind him.

Retreating almost to the Humvee, he saw movement through the sheer curtain over the side-light window.

Ellie's voice called, "It's Johnny. It's Johnny!"

A man's voice came. Harry Keating said, "Open the door."

The lock turned. The door opened.

John stepped cautiously forward again.

Ellie ran out and jumped into John's arms, wrapping her arms and legs around him. "Are you here to rescue us? Has it ended? Is the army with you?"

John laughed as she kissed his cheeks and lips. He noticed her perfume. It came intense and layered, barely covering the smell of sweat. He knew the water supply had failed. There were no baths or showers without running water. John smiled. He hadn't washed either, not for days.

Kathy Keating, the girl's mother, said, "Ellie. Ellie. Control yourself."

Harry, her father, stepped through the door with a shotgun in his hands. He echoed his wife's words. "Control yourself, girl. That there is a fine young man and a blessing of sight." After a look up and down the street, the man stepped back inside and set the weapon into a corner near the front door.

Harry said, "Come in. Come in, Johnny."

Ellie jumped down from John's arms, and she led him inside to stand in the living room.

John noticed the house had a stuffy lived-in odor that had never been there before. They probably hadn't opened any windows or doors for a while. He asked, "Are you all okay?"

"Yes. Yes." Ellie said.

"No injuries? No attacks?"

Harry replied, "A swarm of rioters came through yesterday. They were breaking windows and attacking people on the street. The poor Murray family down the road were beaten up, but nothing before or after that." Harry's tone said the Murray's got worse than he intended to say. The man protected his wife and daughter from the details. The middle-aged man continued, "We keep hearing firetrucks or ambulances. We've stayed inside like the government said for us to do. Then they said to go into the city. We stayed." He lifted his head in strength and confidence. "The power has been off for days. All the neighbors left. They said they were going to be with relatives in Fort Smith or Little Rock. Near as we can tell, we're the only people left on the street."

"Okay. Stay tight. Stay low. Keep the windows shades drawn at night. They don't attack at night. They aren't rioters. They're…"

"What are they?"

"The best word I have for them is zombies."

"No." Harry laughed. "Zombies are in the movies. Can't be a real thing."

John stared at Harry and saw his incredulous, wide eyes.

Kathy's face lost its natural rouge as the blood drained away.

Ellie's lips alternated between a worried smile and a frown. She asked, "Where's your family? Are they in the truck?"

"No. Heading there now but your house is on the way."

Ellie bit her lip. "Have you called them."

"Yes. Once. But the phones are dead."

Harry asked, "You don't know how they are?"

John shook his head.

Harry picked his shotgun up again and said, "Go there. You need to check on them. Do you need food or water?"

"It's just a few miles. I've got what I need." John put his hand on his gun.

Ellie said, "Go there and come back. If they are all okay, bring them here and we can hunker down together until this is over."

"I don't know if they are safe. I'm on my way there." He stopped talking as he fought for the words. "They had to... I told them to board up the windows. The zombies attacked the house." A fake cough covered his choked voice. "The phones are down."

Harry stepped forward. "Go there now." The older man guided John out the front door.

Ellie jumped between them. She pecked John on the lips. "Come back soon. I love you."

John's face turned red. He released Ellie and backed down the steps holding the handrail. He turned on the walkway. The emotions overcame him, and his eyes grew wet. He loved Ellie and was enthralled to know she was secure with her parents, but he needed to know if his family was safe. His memory of the conversation with his mother failed him. They had been attacked. But how badly? He fretted that he'd wasted time at the feed store and again at the pawn-shop. He feared the lost time at the National Guard barricade. John worried he'd spent too much time here checking on Ellie, although he'd needed to, and he was here now. Her house was on the way home.

He walked to the Humvee. His legs took him with speed. He didn't want to rush, but he felt like he needed to hurry. He wanted to go. He needed to go, yet he knew he would be there soon. He needed time. Always too little time.

At the Humvee, he paused and turned back to see Ellie and her family on the steps, watching him.

"Go now, boy," Harry said.

Kathy and Ellie peered at John with lips pressed flat and a slight curve down at the corners.

John lifted a hand to wave, turned, and climbed into the Humvee. As he backed out of the driveway, Ellie raised her hand and blew a kiss from the living room window. He hoped they would close the blinds and stay hidden until he could return. They would be okay. He had hope.

116

Chapter 17 Home Again

'Dog' lay in the grass along the edge of the gravel driveway. It should have barked at the Humvee Cargo-Carrier, but when John stopped and got out, it didn't move. A buzzard landed nearby and hopped towards the pet with flaps of its wings, dropping them to cover its dinner from other carrion feeders. A flock of the birds circled overhead.

"No. No. No." John chased the scavenger.

It flew up, and perched on the tree limb to watch. The circling scavengers moved into the woods to wait.

John scanned the woods with his hand on the holstered handgun, watching for zombies, or worse.

A whimper rose. Dog raised his head and wagged his tail.

"It's all right." John consoled the dying animal. Intestines covered the ground mixed with blood. Grainy, meaty guts and bits of internal organs matted its sunken, collapsed belly fur. No veterinarian could save it. Tears streaked his face as he petted his friend. Great heaving sobs rose.

Dog licked John's hand, wagged its tail in the purest yet short-lived joy. Its pain subsided, perhaps, for a moment as John rubbed its head and face. He stroked under its chin.

John withdrew the Glock and brought the muzzle to Dog's head.

With one last pant and a coughing-gasp, it closed its eyes and died.

"I'm sorry." John re-holstered the gun, grateful that Dog gave up, happy in its last moments. He thanked God he didn't have to shoot it. "I'll bury you by the creek."

He wiped away his tears as he walked towards the

house. Several dead zombies rotted in the grass. John scanned their size and clothing. He didn't recognize any of them. As he walked away from the Humvee halfway along the driveway, birds sang, and crickets chirped–a good sign. The buzzards circled again, high over the sheds–a bad sign. He recalled that where buzzards circled low, they indicated a dead or dying animal, like Dog. This different flock flew above the house, smokehouse, and the shed, a hundred yards up the driveway. When buzzards fly at a higher altitude that meant a human being was injured or dead, but he thought back to recall if he'd seen any birds eating dead zombies. No. They hadn't. For all the people and zombies killed, not one zombie was pecked at by a bird, nor chewed on by dogs or coyotes. He ran around his mother's car and his broken-down pickup truck to find legs protruding from behind the shed.

Pale, white skin and blood on the bared legs brought his run to a stop. One of Janine's shoes lay at his feet. The other shoe hung from her toes, twisted and dirty.

John choked down a scream. He stood frozen, fists clenched, jaw tight, veins in his neck bulging in anger and grief.

The screen door on the back porch slammed. John spun, drew his gun, and aligned the sights on Beau as the man shuffled onto the porch, a beer in his hand. John stifled his instinct to kill his hated cousin.

"Sorry, man." Beau wore a dirty white t-shirt.

"What? What are you sorry for?" John stomped to the steps, lowering the weapon.

"She didn't... When they..." Beau pointed to Janine and gulped at the beer, rivulets running from both corners of his mouth and onto his shirt. He wiped his gullet, missing the froth that dripped from the stubble on his chin. His hands quivered.

John asked, "What happened?"

"The people came…"

"Where's Mom, Sam, and Danny?"

"Inside." Beau turned and went in. John followed. "Aunt Kimberly is sick."

John pushed past Beau and went to his mom's bedroom. He knocked as he opened the door, struck by a horrid odor. "Mom? Mom?"

Kimberly moaned. "Johnny?" She struggled to push herself up on her elbows, failed, and collapsed.

"What's the matter?" He crossed to the bed and pressed a hand to her forehead. She burned. "You have a fever. Have you taken anything?"

"No. No. Don't go outside."

Beau appeared at the door. "She's been talking like that for days."

"What's the smell in here?" It came different, set aside from the corpses outside.

"Sores. Ma has cuts that won't heal. She's turning into a zombie."

John stood and stepped to the doorway in two strides. The men stood nose-to-nose. "If you say that again, I'll kill you."

Beau retreated. "Sorry…"

John muttered, "She's my 'ma,' not yours…" Then he asked, "Where's Sammy?"

"She won't come out of her room."

"Danny?"

"He's sleeping."

Footsteps thumped along the hall. "Is that Johnny?" Danny pushed Beau aside and plowed into his older brother, wrapping his arms around him. "I knew you'd be okay. Mom said you would. Beau didn't think…"

"I'm fine. What happened to Janine?"

"We went out to turn the electricity back on and get some food from the shed-freezer. People came. They ran toward us. I. I..." He cried as his enjoyment switched to grief.

"You did the best you can."

"No. I didn't. I was with Janine when the strangers came out of the woods. I told her to go back into the house. She just stood there and then she ran into the shed. I called for her to run. I tried talking to the people, but they attacked us. I yelled but she..." His voice broke into sobs.

"It's okay."

"I went to get a gun. Beau got a gun. We shot at them, but I don't think we hit them."

John picked up his much younger brother and hugged him. As his shirt grew wet with tears, John stared at Beau.

The man stared at the floor and shuffled his feet. He glanced up, and when their eyes met, Beau looked down again.

Danny's grief subsided, and John carried him up to his room. Beau followed and stopped at the bottom of the stairs.

John set Danny on the boy's bed. John asked, "Stay here for a bit? I'm going to check on Sammy and do some chores. Here. Take this." John drew his handgun and dropped the magazine. He pulled the slide and ejected the round in the chamber and then handed the weapon to Danny.

He leaned in close to whisper in his ear. "You know how to use it and if Beau just happened to catch a stray bullet, say, during a zombie attack, I wouldn't be too upset."

Danny's eyebrows rose. "Okay. But it's not loaded."

John winked. "You better give it back to me then."

The boy's smile turned crooked, and he handed it to

John.

John clapped Danny's shoulder. "Besides. Beau is family, so we probably should shoot him yet."

"Yet." Danny's teeth shined.

"Yet." John went down the steps, passed Beau. "Why don't you fetch some shovels? We gotta bury Janine and the dog."

Beau grunted as he turned and stomped through the house and outside, slamming the door on the way.

Chapter 18 Burial

John's knock on Samantha's bedroom door resulted in her calling out a harsh, "Go away."

"Are you sure!?" John laughed.

Feet hit the floor and footfalls padded to the door. The door flew open. Sammy squinted through sleep-filled eyes. She hugged him. "Johnny. Janine is dead."

"I know. I'm sorry."

"You're alive."

"I am."

She released him and crawled back into bed. "It was hell. The monsters came. They killed Janine. Almost got Danny. We locked the doors. Danny and Beau shot a couple of them, and then we all played dead. Beau said it would be better if we hid and didn't make any noise. The next day we killed a bunch in the yard with the crossbow and the .22. Ran out of ammo. Dog killed four of them before they got him." Tears wet her pajama top. "More came, banging on the windows and doors but they didn't get in. It was like they were playing with us. They banged on the doors like they were trying to scare us. I was scared. We were all scared, but at night they went away."

"There's no corpses outside. No dead zombies." John sat on the edge of the bed.

"Danny and Beau drug 'em into the woods. They stink something awful." She pinched her nose.

"How long has mom been sick?"

"She was sick before you left."

"I didn't notice." John sighed.

"She was worried for you. Didn't want you to know she was ill with you going back to the Army."

"Will she be okay?"

"I don't think so." Her voice dropped, becoming factual.

"Let's pray that she does. We need her."

"I've been taking care of her, but she's speaking gibberish. I've never seen her so bad. I've never seen anyone that sick. Beau says she's turning into a zombie."

"No." John patted her head and brushed her hair from her eyes.

"I hope not, but... We better lock her in. Beau said not to, but..."

"I need you to help with Danny." He dropped his voice to a whisper. "Can you help? Beau is useless."

"With you here..." She nodded.

John went to the shed to find Beau wearing a bandana around his nose and mouth as he pushed a wheelbarrow to Janine's body. He wrestled the corpse, dumping Janine's body into the barrow.

"Gentle," John called. "That's your cousin and my sister."

"She's turned."

"Into a zombie?"

"No. The other kind of 'turned.' "

"Not funny." John retrieved a screwdriver, a hasp, padlock, and screws and returned to the house.

"Are you going to help?" Beau sweated through his shirt as he jammed two shovels and a pick-ax into the wheelbarrow, unceremoniously digging them down beside the body.

John stopped in the shed's doorway and glared at the man before walking to the house.

"Okay. I'll get started. You help when you can." Beau sniggered.

While Kimberly dozed, John screwed the hasp and affixed the padlock to her bedroom door. He kept the door closed and locked anytime he wasn't in the room, and when she awoke, she didn't mention it. He hung the key on a nail by the cellar door.

After affixing the lock, he met Beau by the stream a hundred yards from the house. He found a spot of soft ground atop a small rise with a view of the water as it turned a bend. He'd spent many hours fishing along the rocks and fallen trees near where a beach started and ran south.

The two men buried Janine and Dog, in two separate graves, at John's insistence and to Beau's consternation and considerable effort. Then they led Danny and Samantha to the spot. Kimberly was too sick to come outside. She lay in bed, muttering in her nightmares. John thought she might not know that Janine was dead, and for now, that was okay. "Dear God." He choked on the words as he thought of Mom. He raised wet eyes to Samantha and said, "I can't do it... You need to say something."

"I... I..." Sammy's face turned red as she struggled. "I don't know what to say."

"I'll do it," Danny said, looking at John with his voice cracking and tears streaking his face. Danny bowed. "I'm embarrassed."

"Why?"

"I don't want to cry."

"You cry all you want." John hugged the boy.

"Janine is with God?"

"Yes," Wilcox said.

Danny coughed and said, "Dear God. Janine was a good girl and didn't deserve this. She loved you and prayed every night just like Mom told us to. All she ever wanted in the world was a new dress and for mom to be as happy as she was. Janine was happy. She was thrilled. I don't know why you took her away. I don't know why you turned all these people into monsters but stop it. Amen."

Everyone repeated the closing.

The family walked back to the house that was cast in red as the sun fell low over the trees, and the sky turned amber.

Chapter 19 Mom

Kimberly's condition worsened. With each hour, John watched her weakness grow as he fed her bits of bread dipped in warm soup, heated in a pan on the charcoal grill on the back porch. He gave her antihistamines and wished for antibiotics.

John spent hours with her watching her skin turn grey in the light of a white-gas lantern he'd brought in from the shed. Seeing her eyes sink deeper into dark circles as her adrenal system failed under growing influenza. The bumps on her skin burst and her nightgown became soaked in blood and puss. The sores that didn't seem to heal.

When he peeled the sleeves of her night-clothes back to check the cuts and apply antiseptic and Band-Aids, she cried, "Johnny. No," and, "Leave me alone. I feel so very terrible." She gasped and coughed, and at first, she blew her nose, but as she grew weak, she couldn't hold up her own hands.

"You need to build strength, eat more. You need to get

clean. We need a doctor, but all hell is out there."

"Don't swear," she said through all her sickness–finding her morals and guidance to correct him.

He laughed and departed to fill a pot with tepid water, find a washcloth and soap, and then returned to place them on the nightstand. "Get washed up. I'll find you a fresh nightgown."

He opened her closet and took folded clothing from a shelf, which he draped across the footboard. He lifted her, to mild protest, and set her in a chair. Then he changed the sheets, replacing them with fresh ones from the laundry closet off the kitchen, and left her to her task of changing clothes. When he knocked on the door an hour later, she didn't answer. He pushed on the door and peered in.

She slept in the clean clothing and John knew that if she found the strength for washing and changing then perhaps the illness would pass.

She awoke for a moment. "Johnny?"

He ran the hallway from the living room and asked, "Do you want some more soup?"

"I'm full."

John doubted she could be full, having eaten little. She fell asleep while he watched, evidenced by a deep snore.

Worry cost him his appetite while Beau, Sammy, and Danny chewed on jerky and peanut butter sandwiches.

***

Through the night, while everyone slept, John alternated between sitting on the back porch, walking around the outside of the house with a flashlight, and checking on his mother.

After each time he keyed the padlock to let himself in, he sat on the edge of the bed with a bowl of water and a damp wash-cloth that he pressed to her face and forehead. The water cooled her fever and offered her some relief.

Her snoring turned to the moans of bad dreams. The cold dampness on her face helped her fever, restoring peace to her face and chasing the nightmares away, yet her illness remained unhealed.

John didn't sleep. Until this ended, only vigilance kept him and his family safe.

**

Morning came. The sun shined. The power remained off, and John fired the charcoal grill to make breakfast. Samantha recovered from her shock with grace, offering to cook for the family. As they sat at the picnic table eating fresh eggs from the chicken coup, fried in a pan on the coals, John noticed Beau carried his mother's revolver in a waistband holster.

"Beau. No way."

"What?" The cousin spilled food from his gaping mouth.

"That's my mom's gun."

"She can't use it, and there's…"

"Hand it over."

"I know how to shoot."

"Call of Duty doesn't count."

Beau protested until he sighed and unbuckled his belt, removed the gun and holster, and placed it on the table. John took the weapon and turned to Danny. "You remember everything I told you about shooting?"

Danny nodded and reached for the gun.

John held it back. "What did I teach you?"

He swallowed and said, "It's not a toy. Keep my finger off the trigger until ready-to-fire. Keep it pointed in a safe direction. Always assume it's loaded. Be certain of my target and what's beyond. Never point the gun at anything I don't want to kill."

"Good." John popped the cylinder out and turned the

gun down. "It's empty." Go get the ammo from the hall closet, and I'll show you how to load it."

Danny ran to the house.

"It wasn't loaded?" Beau's mouth fell open again. "You're giving it to Danny? Why does he get to have a gun?"

"Because he knows what he's doing."

"But if the zombies come back…"

"If you want to carry a weapon, get a hammer, screwdriver, or baseball bat from the shed."

"What about gasoline bombs?"

"And burn the house down? Don't be stupid."

"But…"

"You've given me an idea. You know, Beau? You showed me that even an idiot can be useful."

Beau smiled toothily, and Samantha watched as the cousin slowly realized he'd been insulted.

"You need to be a lot nicer to me." Beau glared at John after Danny returned with the ammo and John instructed Danny how to load it.

"Why?" Danny asked. "You're a fish-fart. Why does anyone have to be nice to you?"

John stopped himself from reprimanding the boy. It was hard for John to tell his brother not to insult the cousin he hated so much, even when he should reinforce manners. Doing that would be hypocritical.

Beau said, "Because the whole time you're off playing soldier-boy, I'm here helping Aunt Kim and taking care of these brats, making them breakfast and lunches and doing chores around this place. You abandoned us."

"You know nothing. You drink all my beer. You eat all our food. You don't work. You don't hunt or fish. You don't even do the laundry around here. All that food you eat comes out of mom's two jobs and my Army paycheck."

Beau leaned on his fists. His shoulder rose. "Do you think so? Your mom never cashed one of those checks. She deposited them in your savings account. I work every damn night at the recycling plant. You thought I was out drinking until dawn? I have to walk or hitch to the county dump because I won't ask Aunty for a ride when she gets home so late most nights. The recycling plant is where the money for food comes from, and the rest goes to utilities. So I drank a few of your beers. Tough shit."

"Mom never kept the money?" John's eyes went from his cousin to Samantha and Danny.

Beau said, "No. She didn't. Go inside and check your bank book. It's in the kitchen drawer. You have all your precious money for all its worth in the world. Good luck finding a bank that's open ever again. Every bank, every store is closed forever." Beau faced Danny and threatened the much younger boy, "Don't you ever call me a fish-fart, or milk-toast, or butter-ball, or any other insult ever again."

John warned, "Don't talk like that."

Beau said, "I'm not going to be insulted."

John said, "Don't talk about this not-ending. It's going to stop."

"This is never going to end."

"It will."

"Ha."

John smashed his hand on the table and stood up. "These are little kids. Don't say things like that to them."

Beau stood up from the picnic table and walked tall, shoulders and head upright as he went to the house.

Chapter 20 Bombmaker

That afternoon the electricity returned, lights came on, the refrigerator compressor cycled, and the clock on the stove chirped. Sam and Danny asked to stay up and watch the news. It was the first time John saw them have an interest outside of superhero movies.

He agreed. "We need to find out what's was going on. With electricity, maybe everything will be okay."

He saw their eyes brighten, but he knew the chaos outside didn't form overnight, and wouldn't end soon. He needed a plan.

While they watched TV, John spent hours in the basement between runs to the shed for gasoline, gunpowder from the reloading station, bullets for shrapnel, bolts, and nails, handfuls of gravel, glass jars and beer bottles, and pipe that he cut with a hacksaw. He constructed three pipe-bombs and a dozen Molotov cocktails. Each bomb contained a short fuse, left over from some long past Fourth of July celebration. He stuffed the pipe-bombs in his cargo pockets along with a lighter. The gasoline bombs held an oil-soaked rag. These he placed on a shelf by the basement door, hoping not to need them. They would burn the house down, but he realized they might offer a distraction and protect their escape if they needed to. They would work as the explosives had done at the feed store. He had no plan for where they would go if leaving became necessary.

***

With the kids upstairs playing a game and Beau somewhere, John went to the kitchen drawer where their mom kept their bank, insurance, and other essential papers. He drew out his bank book and flipped it open. There, in old, blue, dot-matrix printer ink was recorded every paycheck he'd received. The numbers showed ever deposit with regularity and listed no withdrawals. He walked to the pantry and opened the door to stare without comprehension at the empty shelves.

Later, he sat on the couch, turned on the TV, and drew his Glock. A button push dropped the magazine. He checked the slide, ejected a round from the chamber, pushed the cartridge back into the magazine, ran the magazine home, cycled the slide again to load the weapon, and placed the gun on the coffee table.

He flipped TV channels. News broadcasts reported from cities all over the country. They all had the same message: *"We restored order. The outbreak of mass insanity is suppressed. After several days..."* A female reporter turned her head from the microphone to look at a gaunt government official standing beside her. Smoke rose from behind the trees of a city park. The autumn colors failed to hide the destruction going on in the city. A dozen police officers, with weapons drawn, ringed the reporter, standing at a distance.

She continued, *"Police are staying on alert, and martial law is still in effect per the governor's orders, even as the President calls for calm in the wake of this national tragedy. I'm here with Little Rock Mayor, Stephen Parish. Mayor, what can you tell us?"*

The reporter held the microphone as the Mayor spoke. *"Order is restored. While we recover from this tragedy, we ask that everyone remain calm. At this time hospitals are operating at full capacity. Anyone who is severely injured should seek help from firefighters, police, churches, or schools. Ask your neighbors. Those with minor injuries are asked to clean the wounds themselves with peroxide or rubbing alcohol and to obey the curfew. Everyone, please remain sheltered in place."*

"Mayor. You can't expect people to care for injuries?"

"If someone is critically injured, they should go to the hospital. Please don't call 911..."

The reporter interrupted. *"Many homes have been burned. People are seeking shelter. We are continuing to get reports of new attacks. Can the city handle this? Is the*

National Guard helping? Can you tell us about FEMA or possibly military assistance?"

"Federal support is coming. As you know, this is a national problem with disturbances in all major cities. All city and county employees are on 24-hour duty until further notice. The National Guard is preparing shelters at the schools and the convention centers. Anyone finding themselves homeless has the support of the city. We provide beds, meals, and other necessities."

"Thank you, Mayor. Can you tell us anything about the cause of the mass insanity?"

"The CDC report indicates a widespread case of media-induced, viral-social-mass-delusions, embedded paranoia, and irrational beliefs, resulting in unacceptable behaviors."

"Mayor, you can't believe that thousands of murders are a mass hallucination."

"No. No. The attacks have stopped. We suppressed the looting. We will arrest criminals. The problems are under control."

John closed his eyes, trying to shake the idiocy of what he'd heard. Sleep took him.

Sammy and Janine went to their rooms while Beau looked for a beer in the warm but recovering refrigerator.

***

John awoke to the sound of a crash. The TV reported another attack. Gunfire rang. A car exploded. He turned it off, yawned, and rolled over on the couch. Sleep came to him again.

***

Samantha screamed.

John leaped from the couch, ran up the stairs and along the hallway. He pushed by Beau–who shuffled toward Samantha's bedroom. John turned the corner into the girl's room.

Kimberly crawled from the floor onto Sam's bed. The girl pushed herself into the corner, kicking at her mother as the woman reached out, clawing the air, grasping, and grabbing at the girl's legs.

John grabbed his mom by her nightgown and pulled her off the bed. The woman screeched as she spun on her knees and fell prone on the floor.

Beau turned into the doorway behind John.

Their mom gained her feet, lifted her head, and growled as she glared at the cousin, then she turned to Samantha again. John stepped between them.

Her milky-white eyes stared into the distance as the woman's anger and adrenaline pumped into her muscles.

John put a hand up and pushed her back as he reached for his gun. "I don't want to kill you." His hand grasped air at his waistband above the empty holster.

"Kill her," Beau yelled from the doorway.

Danny appeared beside Beau. "No. It's mom."

"Kill her," Beau repeated.

"No." Danny kicked Beau in one knee, and when the cousin winced, Danny kicked the other knee. Then he backed away, leaving a furious Beau leaning against the doorframe, rubbing his legs.

Kimberly crouched and drew back. She pulled free of John's grasp, dipped low with splayed legs, and jumped, bouncing off the ceiling.

John stepped sideways as she launched herself. He wound up his fist. As she went by him, arcing, twisting, stretching her arms out toward Sam, he roundhouse punched her in the head.

Her body collapsed on the bed. All control left her muscles as she fell into unconsciousness.

John pulled her to the floor. "It's okay Sam. You are

okay. Mom has a bad fever."

"Get some rope," John called to Danny and Beau. He grabbed Sam's table lamp and yanked out the cord. John used the wires to bind her arms behind her back. He stuffed a sock in her mouth and tied it in as a gag to prevent her from biting her tongue or biting anyone else.

Sam cried. She screamed. She fled out the door, her bare feet slapping the wood of the hall and down the stairs.

**

In the glow of a flashlight, Kim slept with murmurs and moans as John carried her down the stairs and tied her to the bed in her room. He removed her gag, tied her legs to the footboard, and stretched her arms over her head to lash them to the headboard.

When he finished, John retreated from the room and closed the door. It wouldn't latch. The door handle lay on the floor. The door frame hung in splinters.

The others waited in the living room.

"How did she get out of her room?" He asked from outside her door.

No one answered.

He flipped a light switch. The power had failed during the night. He examined the wall with his flashlight. The screws that held the hasp and latch were pulled loose from the wood. Running his palm over the door, he found the door frame splintered. She had struck the door hard, busting it open in a single blow.

He said, "I thought the TV made that noise."

"Mom was going to kill me." Samantha sobbed.

"It's okay now. Mom's tied up. She can't hurt anyone. The CDC is working on this. They're trying to find a cure."

"Mass hysteria," Beau said.

"Bullshit," Danny said.

"Language," John warned and sneered. "It's a virus or

something. She's sick. Just out of her head, a little. She'll be okay." He didn't believe his own words, but he hoped, he prayed he spoke true, and that everyone believed him. "Mom will be okay. Sammy, sleep in Danny's bed tonight with him. Beau, go back to bed."

"What are you going to do?" Beau asked.

"Try to sleep."

Beau said, "You need to kill her."

"No. We need Mom's fever to break. She'll be fine."

"She won't…"

"Shut up, or I'll shut you up."

Beau got up from the couch and tromped up the stairs.

A glint of steel reflected in the moonlight on the floor. The padlock lay open and unlocked. The key protruded from the lock. Wilcox never left it there. He had always stored it on the nail by the basement door. Someone had gone into the room. Someone let Kimberly out. The damage was set-dressing. Someone staged the hasp and door handle. Beau? Why would he go in there in the first place? Perhaps he was wrong. Did Sammy or Danny want to see their mom, or talk to her, or hold her hand, and they forgot to lock the door when they left? Perhaps he'd left the key in the lock by accident and Mom pulled the door handle off and tore loose the hasp. Perhaps.

Chapter 21 Barricades

John walked the hallway several dozen times throughout the night. He stopped at the kitchen door, look out into moonlit fields, turned around and walked to the living room in the front. He looked over larger front pasture and the driveway to the road. The Humvee stood where he'd left it, facing the house, the driver's door still open.

He thought of Ellie Keating. He wondered if she and her parents were safe. He hoped for their lives. These thoughts brought him to concerns about protecting his siblings. He needed to find a cure for his mother.

He returned to the couch to sit for a few minutes. Each time he felt himself dozing off, he awoke anew to the sounds of thrashing and banging in his mother's room. Countless times he thought to put a knife to her head and bury her by the river, beside the graves of Janine and Dog.

The hillock offered a beautiful, peaceful view, one he'd admired when he fished and hunted in the area. If he had to decide on a place for his own eternal rest, that would be it. Mom would love it there, but he was uncertain she'd ever visited the spot, just a few hundred yards out the back door.

Then he recalled how she'd spent summers in the house. She'd said that she inherited it from her grandparents but left it abandoned for several years when he was quite young and returned here when her husband, his father, was killed in action. Wilcox remembered that. They'd left again when she married the gold-digger. He wanted her to sell the place, but she refused. And when he skipped out on her and his condo, they returned here.

She must know the farm and the creek and perhaps many of the trails through the woods and fields. She'd approve of being buried in the clearing.

Each time he stood from the couch, preparing to kill her and bury her, he collapsed, tears streaking his cheeks and nose.

As the night passed, he counted the remaining hours to sunrise as he determined to have her buried before the kids awoke, but, as each hour passed, he couldn't bring himself to do it.

The sun rose, and his grief subsided.

"There'll be a cure. Mom'll be okay," he told himself. "And if it isn't okay? What about Sam, Danny, and Beau?

If she gets out of the room? She won't get out. But what if she did?" The noise subsided in the early morning. He'd begun to doze again but awoke at the total silence.

He went to the door once more and stood, listening. For five minutes, no sound came. Then a sudden gasp of air and the squeak of bedsprings and a fist banging on the headboard came. She was still alive.

If she wouldn't recover, he wished her to die. This in-between monster, this predatory animal became intolerable. He wanted his mom back.

***

Samantha and John prepared breakfast on the grill–venison steaks and the last of the wilting vegetables-a pot of coffee made from water heated in a pan and poured it in phases over the grounds in the electricity-deprived coffee-maker.

John sipped at the coffee-tea with misplaced disappointment. The lack of a decent cup-o-joe seemed most important in this horrid new world. He smirked at his vanity.

Sammy flipped the steaks. "What are you smiling about?"

A thrashing noise came from the woods. Twenty zombies appeared, coming through the brush and ten more approached on the driveway.

"Inside," John ordered.

Samantha pulled the steaks off the grill, and Beau stared.

John drew his handgun. "Now. And stay quiet. Maybe they will pass us by." The family slowly and quietly reentered the house. A rising chorus of howls and guttural groans came as the zombies charged.

John locked the door, but the creatures smashed the glass. Bloody arms bearing oozing sores reached in, grasping, thrashing with long nails. A zombie pulled himself over the shards, ripping his stomach open, sending intestines to the floor. John fired, killing it with a shot to the head.

"Sam, get the shotgun. Danny, Get the deer rifle."

"What should I use?" Beau asked.

"Get a knife."

The zombies encircled the house, ripping at the siding and breaking windows. John moved room to room, killing several as they climbed inside. Heads exploded. Purple blood and gray-matter sprayed.

Beau walked behind John, holding a hammer.

"Do something," John yelled. "Find another room. Use that hammer."

Sammy and Danny screamed. John killed two more zombies in the hallway and ran up the stairs. At the top, Sammy struggled to pull a bedroom door closed as she slashed at a zombie's arms that reached from the bedroom. Danny held Kimberly's revolver in two hands. He took a half-step back, planting his feet, and fired. The zombie died in the threshold, preventing Sammy from closing the door.

John asked, "How did they get up here?" Then he said. "They climbed the lattice on the front porch... How...? Stay behind me." John pushed past them into the room. He killed one zombie by the bed and another climbing in the window from the porch roof. He yanked the body from the doorway and closed the door behind him. John cleared the second floor and made his way down with Sammy and Danny in tow.

In the living room, Beau killed several zombies with a hammer. He stood surrounded by pools of purple blood and dead bodies. "They backed off. I think that's all of them?"

"Backed off? They don't back off. Why would they do that?"

"I dunno." Beau shrugged.

"At the store..."

"Where?" Sam grabbed John's hand.

"I was at a store. We barricaded ourselves inside until we could break out. The zombies didn't leave. We had to escape, but we will be okay here."

"Who?" Sam gripped his hand tighter.

"Huh?"

"Who escaped with you?"

"Devon, Paver, Um..." His memory flashed with images of his friend who was killed by the Guardsman. Images flashed of the battle at the feed store. "It doesn't matter. Three weird people controlled the zombies. They told the zombies who to attack and where to go. Tank-Top killed them with a sniper rifle, but the fight didn't stop. There must have been other controllers."

Beau coughed and asked, "Who do you think is controlling them?"

"Someone in the woods or along the road. That's where I'd be if it were me."

"What do we do about that?"

"Drag the bodies outside. Barricade the windows. Count ammunition. Set a watch. We have work to do."

They cleared dead zombies from the house. They set the corpse in neat rows.

John said, "There's no reason to disrespect the dead. We can't bury them, but maybe they will be buried. Maybe help will come." He said those words, but he didn't believe them. He found no validity in the responses or actions of his family members

When they emptied the house of the dead, they gathered hammers, nails, boards, and plywood to barricade first-floor windows. They nailed slats across the windows inside as well.

John worked hard, Samantha and Danny worked as

best they could, and Beau did as little as possible. They finished near midnight and collapsed into their beds, exhausted.

Chapter 22 Danny

The night passed in a silence devoid of crickets, birds fluttering their wings in their nests, and rabbits, raccoons, and opossums venturing out for midnight meals. The air-itself remained still, too frightened to move, telling a tale of zombies lurking in the woods, not attacking but not dispersing.

Morning came. The sun crested the treetops and in the house laser beams of sunlight cut through holes and gaps in the boards and planks nailed over the windows and furniture stacked against the next zombie attack.

John awoke on the couch, realizing he'd dozed off during his night-watch. He called Danny and Sammy. They didn't answer. He shuffled to the kitchen to pour a cup of cold coffee and found the back door ajar.

From the porch, he looked to the rows of zombie corpses they had removed from the house. They lay in ranks and files. Good people turned bad by disease and killed for their crimes. Arms no longer crossed or at their sides, pointed jaggedly. Legs kicked outward or angled. No longer straight. Clothing was strewn aside. He walked across the grass to see who or what did this and saw pockets turned out. Someone had searched them. Someone was stealing from the dead.

John thought, "Why? What things of value matter? Besides a gun and lot's of ammo for protection, what matters now…? Nothing."

He returned to the house and called for Sam, Danny, and Beau.

Crying came. He crossed the kitchen and living room

and spun to take the steps by twos. The sound came from Samantha's room.

"Johnny? Johnny?" Sam asked.

The girl's voice recalled his mother's tone, how she would holler from the back porch for lunch or dinner, only now, softer, spoken at a whisper–his mother–their mother. Kimberly. She had a name. Kimberly. And she was still alive. Alive and turned. And they had no cure.

"Sam? Are you okay?" He went into her room and moved to her bedside.

"I'm scared."

"It's going to be okay. We're safe. We have food, and..."

"And what?"

He hesitated to say, "Ammunition," but she pressed him, looking for hope. Needing ammunition increase the fear of having it, of needing it. They required ammo, but not for target shooting.

She asked again, "And what?"

"We'll be okay." His voice quivered.

She cried again.

When he sat on the edge of the bed, her shotgun slid sideways and bumped into the nightstand. He picked it up and drew back the slide. A shell, riding on the extractor, withdrew from the breach. The ejector lifted the round, and he picked it out with his fingers. Inside, another shell sat on the ramp. He thrust that home and turned the gun over. Where he should have seen the edge of another round in the magazine, the steel follower glinted from the gun-blued and oiled loading-gate. He pushed the shell in his hand into the tube magazine.

"We're running out..." She pushed herself up.

"Food? There are preserves in the cellar."

"They won't last." She grabbed his hand and pleaded.

"It might be time to take the car and go."

John knew she was right. They ran low on food, and the preserves were mostly sugar and fruit juice, with no protein.

Provided they could keep the zombies out, vitamin pills were limited, the water system ran intermittently and might become contaminated, they needed ammunition, and the zombie bodies would rot, making the air intolerable. One problem at a time. Ammo.

"Do you have any more shotgun shells?" She anticipated his thoughts.

"No? You?"

She shook her head.

"You've two left. One in the chamber." He set the shotgun down again.

She nodded.

He stood, thinking to let her stay in bed if she wished. They had nothing pressing to do but wait for the next attack and plan an escape.

He went to Danny's room–the front bedroom by the porch roof and window–that they'd barricaded since the zombies broke out the glass–and pushed the door open. The boy lay motionless.

John thought to let Danny sleep but something about the child, how he lay perfectly straight on the bed, arms crossed, like the dead zombies outside, concerned him. The boy never slept that way, preferring to flop, exhausted and askew, fallen into unconsciousness from long days of hard play and hard work.

He stepped to the bed and in the dim light saw a dark ring around the boy's neck. "Danny? Danny!" He shook the boy and lifted him from the bed, scooping him up in his arms.

Danny's limp body felt cold in the embrace as his head

lolled and his pale-blue face lolled over to John's chest. Large thick encircling bruises ringed his neck.

"No! No! Who did this!?" He looked to the barred window and the closet as he returned Danny's body to the bed. "Who did this? He's dead."

Footsteps thumped. Samantha came to the door, her face cast in fear, turned to horror. She ran to the bed, but John stepped in front of her to shield her view. He picked her up, but she peered over his shoulder before he could turn. He carried her sideways into the hall.

"Danny's dead?"

John descended the stairs and put Samantha on her feet. "Don't go back upstairs."

The back door closed and Beau came around the corner from the kitchen. A determined walk slowed as he approached the living room.

John asked, "Where've you been? How long was that door open?"

"My shotgun?" Sam ran up the steps.

"Get your shotgun and don't go in Danny's room."

Beau entered the living room at a slow shuffle. His feet slid forward inches at a step.

"What's going on?" The man sipped at a beer can, unable to hide a smirk.

John had thought they ran out of beer for the man seemed to drink often. He stepped closer to his cousin. "How long was that door open? Where were you?"

"Outside. What happened?"

"Danny's dead."

"How?" The man took another sip.

"He was strangled." John stepped forward.

"Zombies?" Beau sipped.

"Zombies don't strangle people."

"They don't?" Sip.

"But you know that." John stared into the man's eyes.

Longer sip. Beau's head tipped down.

John poked Beau's arm. "They pull people apart, rip their arms off. They eat their legs and dive into soft, fat, bellies."

Beau turned.

John poked his cousin's stomach. "They bite their necks, nose, and ears. Use fingers to gouge out eyes and slurp the eye-juice inside." He poked Beau in the face. "They kill people…"

Beau moved back with each poke.

"They   kill people...like…I…am…going…to…kill…you."

Beau bumped into the wall. "No."

"You murdered Danny."

"I didn't."

"You did."

"No."

"He insulted you. You couldn't take the ribbing of children."

"He wouldn't stop…" Beau took another drink.

"He didn't. He said you were lazy, stupid, and drunk."

"All the time."

"Milk-toast."

"All the time."

"Butterball."

"He deserved it."

"He's ten years old."

Beau shrugged.

"You unlocked mom's door."

Beau shrugged again.

"When she didn't come out, you busted mom's door. Let her attack Sammy."

Beau laughed. "That was funny."

John stepped forward, bringing them nose-to-nose, staring eyeball-to-eyeball. "I won't kill you fast. I'm going to kill you nice...and...slow."

Beau turned to escape, but John's hand flashed out to lock fingers around his limp wrist.

When Beau protested, turning back, John connected a fist to the side of his face. The cousin dropped.

***

Beau awoke in darkness. He struggled to move. His arms were stretched, with his wrists tied behind his back. He shifted his legs, finding his ankles bound to the chair legs. He thought. Did someone tie me up? Not Danny, because I wrung the bastard out of the boy and made him a 'good kid.' " He smirked. "Good and dead... No. Not him. Not Samantha either. She's okay but too young for the job. John did it. His memory returned. John punched me after accusing me of killing Danny.

His bound hands struggled to reach the folding knife he kept clipped to a belt loop. He couldn't move his hands far enough, but by twisting and turning, he saw that the knife was missing.

He laughed and thought, "Yes. I throttled the brat out of Danny. I choked him dead. A little boy. Laying there all pleading eyes and rasping gasps, wanting to tell me to stop. Wanting to apologize for endless insults but able to speak because my fingers crushed his windpipe. Oh, how hard it is to breathe with a crushed throat. And it took so long. Minutes. Long enjoyable minutes.

And then there was Janine. She was dead already when I savored that beautiful, sweet, sticky blood. Yes. I hid that. No one saw me when I went out in the dark and ripped a chunk of her arm off with my teeth."

"Well," Beau said to the darkened basement. "I did it. I did it all, and it's not over." He laughed. Big bellowing guffaws rolled from the depths beneath his quivering gullet. Layers of second, third, and fourth chins reverberated. His belly shook.

And he prepared his mind for the next zombie attack.

Chapter 23 Escape

John, with a shovel over his shoulder and handgun on his hip, risked digging a grave for Danny. The boy still lay in his room, waiting for burial.

Twice, as John approached the path leading through the woods to the river, he heard shuffling and the rustle of leaves and brambles. He peered into the thick dark brush, where he'd safely gone before to bury Janine and Dog. He saw nothing at first, but after a dozen yards in, in the distance, in a massive ring around the property, zombies stood shoulder-to-shoulder facing the yard and the house. As if in a stupor, they didn't attack. Gasps, moans, and gurgling, almost talking, came from the creatures.

Since childhood, John memorized every trail and path within miles. He retreated to find another way around. Each way John approached the woods revealed hundreds of zombies surrounding the property. He didn't attempt to conceal himself, yet none of them noticed him.

Uncertainty reigned. John thought of the risk of sneaking around these barely conscious monsters. He, Devon, and Paver had successfully done that to crawl into the parking lot of the feed store and plant the explosives. That was at night. Now was full daylight.

If he went around, carrying Danny's body, the zombies would be between him and the house. He'd left Sam safe if Beau didn't escape the basement, but these things, he knew, may attack at any time. The unreal world-of-zombies transformed to more profound strangeness for he'd only ever seen them standing, rocking side-to-side at night when they appeared to sleep while standing up. The sun neared noon. How could they be sleeping in the daytime?

He went into the house, took several quilts and pressed wool blankets from the linen closet, and went to Danny's room. Samantha lay in bed beside her deceased brother, her arms wrapped around him. She cooed, "I know. You're safe. Mom says you're with Janine. Grandma and Grandpa said everything is going to be okay."

John's heart raced. His face flushed. "Get away from him. You didn't talk to Mom or Grandma or Grandpa. You never knew them. You sound like you're communicating with the dead."

Her words struck John as unnatural, but then he realized how strange life had become, and he regretted his anger.

Sam jumped out of bed. "I... I..."

John sighed. "I'm sorry. I just..."

Sam went to him and took the blankets out of his arms, placed them on the bed, and turned back, wrapping her arms around his midsection. "Everything is going to be okay."

John smiled at the thought of his little sister comforting him, a grown man. She knew. She must see the stress he felt at losing their family and their cousin being to blame. Her concern reminded him again of their mom.

He gently put his hand on her head. "Let's wrap Danny in the blankets. We won't be able to bury him for a while."

"Okay." She released her hug.

They spread out the blankets and wrapped and rolled Danny's body in them. John tied the quilts closed with electrical cords ripped from a lamp and an old alarm clock.

Sam took up her shotgun and moved to the door. "Let's go downstairs and see what we can find to eat."

"I'm not hungry."

"We have to eat, and then we'll leave. It's almost dark. We can take the car."

"What about Beau?" John asked, not sure he wanted Sam to think about what their cousin did.

"Kill him. Put a bullet in his head."

"Sam!?"

"What?" She turned back.

"I shouldn't have asked, but you want me to kill him?"

"He murdered Danny. He deserves it. Eye-for-an-eye. Like it should be." A tiny shrug rose and fell.

"But?"

"I'm not going to do it. You are."

"I wasn't going to ask…"

"Just do it." Sam walked down the stairs.

"What about mom? She's too sick to travel."

"Shoot her too."

"I can't kill Mom."

"She's not 'Mom' anymore. She's one of them."

"I… I can't…"

John grabbed a flashlight from the kitchen and followed her to the basement. "Slow down," he said. "If he got loose…"

She retrieved her flashlight from a pocket and turned it on. The beam reached into the darkness to land on Beau.

"He's still tied-up."

***

Outside, in the fading grays and muted shadows of the sun setting in a cloudless sky, a chorus of wails rose from behind every bush and tree.

Moving en masse, the zombies ran, tripped, picked themselves up, and staggered toward the house.

***

John and Sammy froze, waiting, listening to the sound of the ground shaking, reverberating as if heard from underwater. Dust fell from the beams and joists of the dark basement as claws dug into the clapboard siding, tore at barricaded windows, and pounded on the doors. A splintering of wood cut at their eardrums.

The sound of footsteps came from over their heads.

Sammy gasped. "They're getting inside. What do we do?"

John ran up the steps. "I'm going for Ma."

"Don't. It's too late. Mom's turned," said Samantha as she followed John.

"I can't leave her to be attacked by them. She's going with us, sick or not. Bolt this door behind me. Count to thirty. If I'm not back then leave Beau tied up and escape out the cellar door. The keys are in the Hummer."

"You're not leaving me."

John said, "I'll be back in twenty seconds. If you hear me calling, then open the door. If you hear me screaming…"

"I won't open it!"

Footsteps shuffled in the night-darkened kitchen as John went through the door. He heard Sam lock the slide-bolt behind him.

A zombie reached for him through the beam of his flashlight, and he stepped back, raised his gun, and shot it in the head. Brains splattered across the cabinets and dirty dishes on the countertops. He sprinted to his mother's bedroom.

Through the half-opened door, he found her thrashing in convulsions of anger and rage, trying to escape the electrical cords and ropes that tied her down. She gnashed her teeth, biting at the air, and fingers repeatedly stretched wide and curled into fists, pulling against her bonds.

The adrenaline in his system fell away. He stood staring, realizing that this is how zombies were created.

They were sick, brain damaged, uncomprehending. She'd become a monster. She'd turned into a rager, and there was no cure. There would never be a cure.

He placed the handgun to her head and pulled the trigger, ending her torment. There would be no other treatment. Her pain stopped.

A zombie came into the bedroom. John shot it dead.

He went into the hallway again and looked right and left. A dozen zombies moved through the living room. He killed three of them and ran to the kitchen. He aligned the gunsights and dispatched two more coming in the back door. At the top of the basement stairway, at the door, he said, "Let me in."

Sammy unlocked the door and fled down the steps. "I heard gunshots."

John saw the small family photograph hanging in its frame over the kitchen table.

He said, "Mom's dead." He took two long steps and grabbed the picture off the wall and stuff it up under his shirt.

Sammy said, "Now shoot Beau. He deserves it."

"No. I'm going to kill him slowly." After locking the door behind him, he descended the steps three at the time. "That won't hold. We've got to get out of here."

"What about Danny?"

John hesitated and then said, "We can't... We'll have to come back to bury him."

Zombies banged on the cellar door. The wood cracked.

Beau whined, "Don't leave me here."

Sam pointed a flashlight at Beau. "Shoot him."

"He's coming with us." John flicked open his pocketknife and cut the ropes holding Beau's ankles to the chair legs. He cut the cords that held Beau's arms to the chair-back but left their cousin's wrists secured. "Get up."

Beau rose as John pushed him toward the cellar bulkhead door to the side yard.

Beau asked, "What about the zombies outside?"

"They'll all be inside the house in a minute, and I have a surprise for them."

Sam slid the bolt on the rusted steel bulkhead door.

John said, "Hold on. Douse your flashlight."

Her light flicked off. "What?"

"Shhhh. We'll wait for them to come down the stairs." He returned to the inside stairs and lined pipebombs from his pockets on the steps. The gasoline cannister was set beside the workbench.

The door up the stair splintered and wails came through the cracks.

John grabbed the gas can and poured a line from the steps to the bulkhead.

Zombies stumbled and fell as they came down.

"Go. Go. Get to the car." John tossed down the can and fished a lighter from a pocket.

Sam opened the bulkhead door, and Beau followed her outside.

John dropped his flashlight and lit the gasoline trail. He lit the fuse on the third bomb and threw it inside as he stepped into the night.

He ran after Sam and pushed along the lagging Beau. "Move it, Beau. Do you want to be torn apart?"

Beau said, "Better than tortured by you."

"Get going."

The bombs exploded as zombies reached the top of the bulkhead steps, their clothes burning from the gasoline. The fire billowed, engulfing the zombies. The basement burned, setting the entire hour alight, killing all the zombies within it. On the first floor, through doorways and windows, the zombies flooded back outside, unthinking, not to escape the flames, but to follow their prey.

Sam reached the car. John opened the back of the Humvee's cargo box. "Sammy, you drive." He tossed the keys to her.

"This is a military truck."

"Same as my pickup. You know how to drive."

She got inside and started the engine.

John shoved Beau. "Get in."

Beau said, "Not in there."

John pushed the man over the pintle hitch and bumper, and hoisted him inside, slamming the cargo box-door closed. John jumped in the passenger side and slammed the door. Sam already had the car in reverse. She let off the brake and took them, driving backward, down the driveway to the road.

The view out the windshield showed zombies coming after the Humvee. The fire set in the basement raced through the ancient wood structure to cast the zombies in silhouette.

John said, "Lights."

Sam searched for the switch and found it. The headlights illuminated the zombies.

She sped-up as they approached the ditch by the road. When the rear tires grabbed the pavement, she cut the wheel, stomped on the brakes, and threw the shifter into drive. The front end spun around.

"I never taught you to drive like that." Wilcox gave her a grin. "How'd you learn the drive like that?"

She said, "Video games."

The family home burned behind the mass of zombies. Danny's and Kimberly's unburied bodies were abandoned, cremated in their beds, burned to ash in their house. There would be no memorial service. No one would bury them or give them last rights. The two siblings paid the price in guilt for their lives.

John drew the family photograph from under his shirt and placed it in the well between the front seats of the Humvee.

Chapter 24 Little Rock

The Humvee rolled along Whitwell Street, pushing through clouds of smoke and glowing airborne cinders darting towards the windshield and sweeping up or around at the last moment. The neighborhood burned. Half the houses glowed red with burning embers where the flames subsided and left empty shells standing where homes once sat. Trees burned with the cracks and pops of their sap boiling inside. The fires all around heated the Humvee such that John rolled up the windows. He drove with two feet on the pedals, ready to accelerate forward, or brake and reverse away from trouble.

He counted the houses and tried to remember the one that Ellie's parents owned. In the light of the fires and through the choking haze, he struggled the home. Everything burned or had burned out. Cars smoldered in the driveways. Mailboxes cooked. Telephone poles had turned to ash or broken off, leaving behind strewn wires that were devoid of power. Landmarks were missing from where trees once stood, and where the whites, and greens, and reds of house paint had changed to blacks and greys, and destruction.

He stopped.

"What's going on?" Sammy suddenly looked around, as if awoken from a daze.

"Ellie's house." John stepped out of the truck.

Sammy looked from each shell of a house or foundation to the next, up along the street, and then back the way they came.

She said, "I'm sorry, Johnny."

John walked to the curb, looked right and left, took a few steps towards a sedan in a driveway, stopped, and turned back.

"They aren't here." He hoped they weren't. He'd hoped they'd fled before the fires came. The burning car sat in what seemed to be their driveway, unrecognizable. The whole street was unrecognizable.

He turned away from the scene, wiped tears from his eyes, and sat in the vehicle silent, unmoving and trying unsuccessfully to be unmoved. He couldn't tell Sammy of his thoughts. She was too young.

He held inside all of his guilt, blame, accusations, and self-accusation. Thoughts and emotions mixed like protein powder in a shaker bottle. His brain rattled with the clack, clack, clack of a metal mixer: Shit happens; They'll be okay; They must have left; No one would stay in a house on fire; No one would stay with their neighbor's houses on fire and spreading; The zombies must have come through and torched everything; One house burned and they all caught fire; The grass and trees are dry from a drought; Maybe it wasn't zombies; Could have been an accident; Someone left a stove on when they abandoned their house; Maybe someone left a toaster plugged in, and on, when the power returned for a few minutes. Did a piece of paper left on top catch fire? Did cabinets above heat up and ignite? Did food in a cupboard burn? Once started, it spread like the zombie swarms. All the houses burned. They left. That's not their car. They would have gone... Where? Somewhere safe. The stadium? No. The woods? They weren't survivalist. A relatives house? Yes. They'd go somewhere safe. Yes? They must have. He turned and stared at the burned car in the driveway, at the burned trees and powerlines, and the foundations where houses once stood. He counted the driveways, the gaps in the curbs. How many homes from the corner? Why couldn't he remember? Which house was it? How many cars did they have?

Sammy unbuckled her seatbelt and turned and half-rose from the bucket seat. She slid over to John's side, hugged him, and said, "I'm sorry." She repeated the words. She repeated the words she'd said before. They didn't help. No words offered help.

***

An hour later, they used the elevated highway that passed through the city of Little Rock. The town burned in yellow, orange, and amber through endless clouds of smoke. A siren wailed, rose, gave an agonizing screech, and died. Distant thunder came in waves. It rose and fell, not from the sky, but from collapsing buildings, burning trees, and machine gun fire.

An Airforce jet turned in a tight arc around the city. It straightened, angled down, and drove towards the ground. It unleashed four rockets, and fired machine guns into the NFL stadium, then pulled up as the bombs exploded. A giant mushroom of fire rose into the sky. Thirty seconds later four more fighter jets followed the first, unleashing tracers that marked their path into the open roof of the sports complex, one after the other. The mayor, the governor, and newscasters had told people to gather for safety there, and now everyone was dead or burning alive. But they wouldn't have killed uninfected people? He wondered if zombies overran the place and someone called in the strikes. Why didn't the Governor tell people to go there? Because the Air-Force wouldn't have been able to keep the infected out or separated. He remembered the phone calls from Fort Leonard Wood.

The fighter jets departed to some distant air-base

surrounded by chain-link fences and protected by guns firepower. Wilcox saw the lights of a C130 circling the stadium, door-gunners fired into the flaming structure.

His heart grew cold and beat slower with an icy rage as he wondered if Ellie might have gone there. He punched the steering wheel.

Sam yawned. Her exhaustion was so complete that the world of war and horror couldn't keep her awake. "Where are we going?"

"Fort Leonard Wood." He steered around broken-down cars on the highway.

"Shouldn't we go to the stadium or the police?"

He looked across the city. He pointed. "Hard to imagine anyone's alive out there."

Sam said, "The zombies don't come out at night."

"Except tonight."

"Yeah… Wouldn't the stadium be safer?" Her words slowed.

He ignored her. She didn't see or recognize the city or its landmarks. She was too young. "The fort has guns, guards, and barbwire." He recalled the frantic calls the fort made to him, Devon, and Paver. "I hope…"

"What?"

"Nothing."

"How long until…" Her head fell forward, and she dropped into sleep again.

Beau, who spent the first half of the journey whining and complaining, had fallen quiet again. John couldn't remember if Beau complained as they drove along Whitwell Street. He didn't care if the boy cooked in the back of the cargo area from those flames.

Beau complained again, and his voice roused Sam. She'd slept for less than a minute.

"Shut up," John ordered.

"Huh?" Sammy rolled her head and eyes.

"Beau." John threw a thumb over his shoulder.

"Oh." She leaned her head on her hand, elbow propped against the window.

Wilcox turned a curve in the highway. A dozen zombies blocked the way. The monsters stood in their familiar swaying sleep-like state.

In the darkness, John couldn't see beyond them and didn't dare run them down and risk getting the wheels or axle stuck on top of their bodies. He locked the brakes.

The zombies turned to face them. Several ran to a car, while others crouched and leapt like baboons, coming on fast. Still other's picked up debris to use as a weapon. One swung a detached car-bumper. John accelerated. The Humvee ran them down.

Beyond the first group, a score of other zombies charged in to attack the vehicle. Wilcox swerved into them, sending bodies flying.

Beau whined. Sam screamed.

The road opened. John drove a quarter mile and then stopped.

He called to Beau. "Did you enjoy killing an innocent little kid? You murdered Danny. You infected Mom. You called in zombies to kill Janine when she..." He paused, imagining his littlest sister and Danny running to the shed for food and the zombies coming out of the woods. Danny had barely escaped. Janine had been torn apart like so many others. He'd seen that at the bus station, at the farm store.

John asked, "Beau, what would a zombie do to you?" He got out and walked to the back of the vehicle, casting an eye to the distance behind them and hearing the zombies following, catching up. He opened the cargo bay door.

"Wait. Wait," Beau said. He twisted around with his wrists still firmly bound behind his back.

"This is where you get out." John lifted the man and hoisted his bulk out of the car.

Beau flopped out with a grunt.

As John climbed into the driver's door and shifted into drive, the zombies closed in. In the moonlight, in the mirrors, John and Sammy watched the zombies stop, surround Beau, and stand beside Beau. One of them reached down with a machete and cut Beau's wrists free.

Beau rose. He laughed. He stared after the Humvee.

"Controller." John slammed on the brakes, stopped, and looked at Sam. She unlatched her lap belt and knelt on the seat, looking back.

She asked, "Control what?"

"Zombies."

"Kill him."

John shifted into reverse and stomped on the gas peddle. The last John saw of Beau was his outstretched hands, trying to stop the vehicle as it crashed into him. The cousin went under the wheels, crumbled, crushed, and rolled underneath with several zombies. Crunching, snapping, and squishing sounds joined a burst from under the floorboards.

As the car cleared the group, and a jumbled mass of blood, guts, and bones sprayed up into their headlights, John slowed.

A dozen zombies attacked the vehicle from the sides.

"They don't attack without command. There's another Controller." John looked for the other human who directed the zombies.

"Where?" Sammy looked around.

"We're not going to find out." He put the shifter into drive and ran over the bodies again.

Sammy said, "Kill Beau again… For good measure."

They escaped onto the open highway. A few miles up the road, they slowed and weaved through and between abandoned cars. In the darkness, the headlights illuminated the camouflage-painted MRAP-Badger. The closed doors indicated Paver's body hadn't been disturbed.

John stopped and recalled his friend. He talked to Sammy about the man, remembering times in Basic Training, and studying together at demolition school. A few months of being classmates, teammates, and drinking associates seemed like a lifetime's worth of friendship. "Paver didn't deserve that."

She awoke. "Who?"

She hadn't heard him. He'd spoken only to himself.

John smiled at his memories and didn't answer Sammy as he drove around the vehicle that kept Paver's body safe.

Chapter 25 Sammy

John told Sammy to wait in the car while he cleared and secured a dollar store. Three zombies stood inside. Each of them wandered listlessly, with no direction and no anger or violence toward him. They died silently and quickly on his blade.

He called Sammy inside and closed the steel security doors.

They built a campfire using bundles of firewood taken from the garden center. Wilcox stacked extra wood in the middle of an aisle as Sam 'shopped' for food.

Their meal cooked on a steel rack propped over the flames. The smoke dissipated into the vast high ceilings of the store.

Their midnight dinner consisted of frozen hamburger patties, thawed when the power had failed, potato chips, and warm soda. Sam gobbled down bags of gummies and half-melted chocolates.

After they'd eaten their fill and the fire fell to embers, John grabbed blankets from a shelf. Sam gathered stuffed animals form the toy section to use as pillows.

She handed him a giant stuffed elephant. "Are we safe in here?"

"Yeah. We'll be okay. When this all started Devon, Paver and I found a farm store. We were safe there for a while..." Remembering his friends forced him to recall the loss of their family. Tears filled his eyes.

Sam moved to put her arms around him.

"I'm okay," he said.

"It's okay to cry." Her soft, young voice consoled him.

John's heart cracked. He put an arm around her, hugging her back, knowing that he should be the strong one. He should be comforting her, but having failed to protect his family from his cousin, doubt filled his mind. If only, he thought, he'd come home sooner instead of spending days in Branson. If he'd worked the factory job as his mom wanted, he could have hunted in the fall and fished all year. They'd have more food, and he'd have been home to protect his family from Beau.

Beau. That evil, dead fucker. His grief turned to quiet anger. A smoldering fire burned within him.

Sam held him tighter, and they drifted to sleep, older brother and younger sister.

***

The morning sky shined through skylights in the roof. John awoke. He gathered non-perishables for the remainder of the drive, collecting canned food, cereal boxes, pasta, and sauces. He filled a dozen grocery bags and put them in a cart that he pushed around the store. The market had been picked through by looters, but much was left, the thieves had taken the candy and left behind the healthier foodstuffs. They'd eat well on the journey and whatever they had to give to the cooks at the fort might buy Sammy's way in. It might forgive for his failure to report in–if they made it that far, if they survived, and if there was anything or anyone there. They had nowhere else to go. He didn't know if they would let Samantha come with him, but he knew guards might take bribes. Maybe. He had never gone AWOL when the world fell apart.

***

Sam awoke to scratch her arms and felt dried blood sticking to her blouse. She pushed up her sleeve and inspected a wound. It itched. She picked at it.

Blood flowed anew.

John turned the aisle and saw her. "What's that?"

Sam pulled the sleeve down.

He left the cart and asked again, "What is that?"

"Nothing."

He dropped the bags and fell to his knees at her side. She pulled away as he took her arm. His grip held her tight, and he raised her sleeve.

"No. Don't."

A bruise ringed the bleeding teeth-marks of a bite.

"Don't." She pulled away.

He released her. "Why didn't you tell me?"

She shook her head.

"I'll get peroxide."

"It won't help."

"Sam. Sam. We've got to treat it. You could die. You could…"

"It's too late."

"No. NO!" He stood and turned to run down the aisle.

Her voice came soft, resigned. "Johnny?"

He stopped and slowly turned to walk back to her.

"I can feel the virus. My head is stuffing up. There's a fire in my blood. Worse than before."

"When did it happen…?" John sat down beside her.

"A couple of days ago, when they attacked the house."

"Let me help you. We'll find antibiotics, medicine, whatever it takes."

"There's no cure."

John stood again. "I'm getting a first aid kit. I'll clean the wound, and then we find a pharmacy. Okay? There's got to be a pharmacy in the store."

She didn't answer.

"You can beat this. The virus doesn't kill everyone. Some people control zombies. Some are immune. No virus kills everyone."

She didn't respond.

"Say okay."

She shook her head.

"Samantha. I need you to know this will be okay. Say it."

"Okay." She nodded. Her jaw tightened, and a stiff smile rose.

John realized that forced cheer was a hope, but he wanted more. He needed her to know that she might survive. He wanted a cure. Maybe if he, or she, or God, had to choose, she might control the zombies, like Beau, like Cart-Woman, and the three controllers in the parking lot at the farm store. At least she would be alive. He gulped a sob. If she controlled them, she would be alive. Then everything would be okay. And then doctors and scientists could find a cure.

"Okay." He patted her head and stood, running to locate a first aid kit. He scanned the aisles, row after row, and shelf after shelf.

A gunshot echoed through the store.

An empty cartridge casing skittered.

A gun clattered.

John froze.

His hand went to his empty holster, remembering he'd placed the weapon on the store shelf before he slept.

"No. No. No. No..." His feet took him faster than he'd ever run.

The side of her head oozed.

He turned the corner and there she lay, where he had left her, feet from the shelf where he'd put the handgun. The handgun on the floor, blood flowing around it.

He fell beside her and brushed the hair from her face, tentatively daring to touch her–frightened for her lifeless eyes. He closed her eyelids with shaking fingers, horrified that they opened halfway-again on their own. Peace and contentment returned to her face as her twelve years slipped to the innocence of a baby or a toddler. Her tense and strained face went slack. Her dark, sunken eye-sockets lightened. The fragile china-doll lay cracked, broken, serene, and peaceful. The little girl slept forever, dreaming of happy days, playing in the woods by the stream, playing with Dog, and Janine. Holding Mom's hand. He wanted her to be like she was before the zombies came.

He took her in his arms and held her close. burying his face in her neck, his hand brushing her bloody head. He shook. Tears fell into her hair and on her blouse to mix with her blood. He cried until he sobbed. His sobs rose to wails. His wails dropped into silence.

He released her, gently setting her down on her blanket. He put a stuffed bear under her head. He put her hands across her chest, forming a cross and then decided to place her hands together, fingers interwoven as if in prayer, he then tucked a plush toy tiger into the crook of her arm.

Fingers closed around the gun that ended his sister's

162

affliction. The muzzle pressed to his temple offered them reunion. He vowed to go to Mom, Danny, Janine, and Sammy. He wanted to pet Dog and hand it a bone. He cried again. His breath came shallow and fast. His hands trembled. He steadied himself, took a deep breath, and tightened his grip. He aligned the muzzle to his ear.

***

Inside the weapon, under the tension of his fingertip, the trigger safety released, and the lever rotated. A steel bar slid back to unlatch the striker. The coil spring released its tension. Kinetic energy slammed the striker forward, hitting the cartridge primer. The force ignited the potassium perchlorate, sending flames through the primer hole to the main charge, but the gunpowder did not burn. The cartridge didn't fire. The gun didn't go off.

No bullet killed John.

His thick, soul-crushing wail returned until he remembered that Ellie might still be alive. He might find her. He had to try.

The End.

Excerpt from *Rayzor: Zombie War Series* Book One.

I killed a puppy - murdered it, actually. I shot it right between the eyes with a gun and didn't feel even a little remorseful. It didn't bother me. In fact, at the moment of pulling the trigger, it was the right thing to do.

My long hair stuck to my cheek as I awoke in tears. I couldn't remember when I last cried, perhaps a year before when my mother died of the virus. I slowed my breathing to avoid waking anyone else in the dormitory.

Sleep escaped me. To pass the time, I listened to the sounds of the hospital we called 'Fort Tulsa.' Through the barricaded windows set high-up in the warehouse-barracks, the September sky forewarned of the morning. The night patrols would be back, and maybe my boyfriend would return from his mission.

Corporal Jim Barnett, with his square-jaw, brown hair, and dark hazel eyes, deeper than my own brown eyes, was handsome in the way a man can be but a boy cannot. He stood tall, carried a strong man's frame, and employed a tender man's voice. He was two years older than me, but I didn't worry about that.

He'd departed with the Lieutenant-Colonel and three squads. Long overdue, three days had passed with no word on the military radio. I missed the man who went off to help defend Tulsa from the zombies, and the boy who pulled my ponytail before we started dating. I tried to forget that his patrol risked zombi attacks all the time. The war had entered its second year.

The snores of Private John Wilcox, our resident explosives specialist, and all around red-neck jerk echoed from the men's side. The sound carried through the twenty-foot tall wall of shelves separating the men from the women. Wilcox wouldn't let anyone forget him either awake or asleep.

His short fiery hair stood in tribute to his temper. Even his snores sounded angry, but the nasal resonance seemed off. I wondered if Wilcox dreamed of new vulgar jokes and laughed in his sleep or perhaps he killed zombies in his fantasies for doing it in the real world appeared never enough for his battle lust. With each snore, a little creak or scratching noise came. Perhaps other soldiers or civilians in the makeshift dorm snored in sync? Did rats work with nasal acoustic protection? Listening again for the sound, it stopped.

I turned on my cell phone and used it as a flashlight. (No one had phone service anymore.) I looked across the room at hundreds of army cots, hospital beds, double and triple-decker bunk-beds, hammocks, and sleeping mats in the former city hospital warehouse. Half the beds were empty. Excluding night shift guards and civilians who slept during the day the vacancies indicated the toll that the virus had taken.

My right leg itched. I retrieved a straightened coat hanger from my nightstand table and slid it down between my leg and the plaster cast on my broken shin bone.

The cast, intolerable from the moment Dr. Teresa Scarbrough, a former general practitioner, and Felix Vinson, our full-time zombie researcher, applied it, encumbered my movements and itched constantly. I had asked for a walking cast. Felix brushed his long brown hair from his face. "That was before the zombies." His nasal laughter had risen. "No one gets anything like that anymore."

Felix played the nerd, including his crush on me, but

his humor made me want to vomit. Literally, throw up. The day I broke my leg, he'd scolded me for carrying a stretcher down the stairs. That day, Jill Addison my blonde-haired, blue-eyed, mid-western, California-girl, best friend and I moved a patient for surgery. I stumbled on the steps, and the stretcher plowed over the top of me. The patient went for a wild ride down the stairs, and I snapped a shin bone in an instant.

Jill and I had laughed as I lay on the floor at the bottom of the stairs. I'd felt no pain, but when I tried to stand up, our laughter ceased.

Jim Barnett came to see me as I nursed the leg. Our banter grew during those weeks. We had our first kiss. He brought me meals. As I healed, he walked with me to physical therapy.

The scratching returned in perfect rhythm to Wilcox's snores. I wondered if the zombies tunneled beneath the hospital.

The scratching sounds didn't come from that side of the warehouse, but from the air vent under the stairs.

I reached for the .44 caliber revolver under my pillow. With annoyance, I remembered how Felix confiscated it when he'd escorted me to my bed.

"Ms. Ray-zor," I recalled the sinus pitch of Felix's voice as he scolded me. "Teenagers aren't allowed to have weapons."

He knew I hated that. Everyone knew I hated having my name drawn out like that—RAY-Zor or worse, Raz. I'd told Felix I'd been shooting since I was eight years old. I'd told him the gun belonged to my dad. He told me he'd check it into the armory alongside my dad's Model-12 shotgun, taken when I first arrived at Fort Tulsa. Everyone also knows everyone carries a handgun. Everyone keeps them hidden, and they know they shouldn't get caught by the guards with one. Jim Barnett's eyes had rolled to the ceiling at Felix's stupidity.

I swung my leg-cast over the side of the bed, being careful to be silent when it touched the floor. My cell phone flashlight went to sleep, so I woke it up. A glint of metal came from a pocket of my jeans on the nightstand. Jim had told me he couldn't get my .44 back, but he gave me a .32 Walther PPK semi-automatic handgun. He hid it in my jeans pocket for 'just-in-case.'

Pulling the jeans on, I cringed at the long slice up the leg that Felix cut to fit over the cast. Still pissed off about the damage to my last good pair of jeans, I had mended the gash with safety pins. I threw a scarf around my neck to ward off the virus rather than for warmth.

With the .32 in hand, I slipped the slide back just enough to see the brass of a cartridge inside. A round of ammunition sat in the pipe. I dropped the slide and clicked the safety latch to red.

My flashlight went out again. The sound of the scratching grew louder as I approached a ventilation grate beneath the stairs. I timed the landing of my cast on the floor to the rhythm of the scratching, trying to cover the sound of my footsteps. The noise sped up, and rapid breathing joined in. My heartbeat thumped like a drum. Sweat soaked my shirt. The raspy breath turned to a whine.

I knelt down at the grate. My flashlight-phone gleamed in the eyes of a puppy stuck inside the vent. Feral dogs were rampant in the Tulsa wasteland, but he appeared young, cute, playful, and black. I love black dogs, always wanting one, this seemed to be a Labrador mixed with German-Shepherd.

I sat down to turn the latches and raise the ventilation grate to let the puppy free. It scratched at the floor and jumped into my lap, tail wagging in joy at his release. The grill fell out of my hands, landing with a clatter. A noise like a runaway-train-on-fire rose from the vent. I stood and backed away, holding the puppy close and pointing the gun at the grate.

"Christ," someone yelled. Footsteps approached. The soldiers that patrolled the hospital were coming. Flashlights came on around the room.

Corporal Gary Lopez ran up to me, the flashlight on his carbine flickering light around the room.

"What is it?" he demanded.

I sighed, not wanting to a hassle. Lopez would give me crap over the dog. I knew it.

"Did you open that vent?" Lopez bellowed at me. His pale blue eyes almost glowed in the dark. His voice rose so loud that people started to wake up.

"It's just a puppy." The puppy growled and tried to bite me. Green and yellow puss oozed from its mouth as it attempted to sink small, sharp teeth into my arm. Did the enemy create an infected dog? Lopez shined his flashlight on red filled eyes. The blood inside left them blind.

Excerpt from *RayzorWire: Rayzor Zombie War Series* Book Two

Leaping from the bed, I grabbed my cell phone to use as a flashlight while I pulled my pants and shirt on.

Lopez awoke.

"Turn that light out," he demanded.

"That was gunfire," I said as I jammed my feet into my boots.

"What?"

Another burst of machine gun fire echoed through the house. Boots stomped up the stairs as yelling filled the air between Claymore mine explosions. We were discovered by zombies or worse; Scabs.

I grabbed my gun belt and shotgun and headed for the stairs. Jim and Jill were already there, calling down to Escobar and Wilcox.

The gunfire was deafening, but between the bursts, I heard Wilcox yelling, "Zombies. Get down here and help."

I pushed past Jill and Jim and scampered down the steps to the second-floor balcony overlooking the living room, grabbing the gasoline can as I went. The others followed behind me.

Escobar and Wilcox came up from the first floor, shooting into the foyer as blind and enraged zombies filled the house. We lined the balcony with guns roaring. The front door was closed but shook as zombies pounded violently upon the wooden slab from the outside. Inside, the hallways below us were filled with half-clothed and sharp-clawed zombies.

These were not the washed and prepped, new civilization of zombies wearing clean clothes and well-fed on prepackaged foods that we normal encountered in Tulsa. These were a different tribe; old-school, bloody, dirty, torn flesh, green and yellow sores oozing puss, swollen purple abscises threatening to burst and spread the virus.

"Peace. Stop. Calm. Stay," I commanded the Zomb with my own thoughts. They didn't listen.

"Betrayer," a leader spoke to me.

"Kill her," many Leaders said in unison.

"There," I yelled. "A Leader." I shot him… or it. The zombies didn't stop their attack, being driven along the hallways and guided up the stairs.

As I lifted the can of gasoline a zombie came towards me, looking at me and almost smiling, his eyes filled with blood, red… almost purple, but somehow possessing clarity, these eyes moved, maybe only half-blinded. It looked at me. It was not a Leader and not a brain-damaged zombie, but something, somehow, caught between the two - a half-zombie.

His... its... thoughts broadcast, "Kill. Kill. Kill," as I tossed the can of gasoline into its arms. Firing my revolver, I blasted bullets through the can, five in and five out the other side and into the zombie. As gasoline poured like a fountain from the holes, soaking the creature's clothing and flowing down the stairs at his feet, he continued to stare at me with comprehending eyes and something new... something I never witnessed before in these monsters... fear.

"Wilcox. Do you smoke?" I glanced over my shoulder and then looked back at the half-zombie standing before me.

"Not now, Raz," he replied as he stood beside me and drilled zombies below us.

"Lighter. Ignite the gasoline. Now." The acrid fumes singed my nostrils.

"The gunfire will do it."

"Not soon enough. Do it now." The zombie stared in horror and fear, realizing my words. I wondered if he knew how we felt. I reached forward and pushed the zombie down the steps, and I backed away. It tumbled into the claws of three more zombies starting up the steps.

Wilcox lowered his gun as he fumbled through his pockets for his Zippo lighter. Recovering the lighter, he struck the flint, and the yellow flame grew. Tossing it onto the stairs, he created a wall of fire that filled the air. Raging heat pushed us backwards. Sweat on my hands dried instantly. The skin tightening on my cheeks burned like fired glass. I blinked, stepping back as we retreated down the hallway. Zombies engulfed in flames continued to come at us. More zombies entered the fire at the direction of the Leaders, those uncaring drovers of slaves. I wondered how I could be associated with them in any small way.

We backed into a bedroom at the end of the hallway. The zombies following, burning, wailing in pain, claws reaching, bodies bleeding from bullet holes in their chests that slowed them down but did not stop them. Shots to the head killed them, and the fallen zombies blocked the way for the others who crawled over the pile of their own burning dead.

"Where did they come from?" Jill cried out as she fumbled to reload her shotgun.

"The basement," Escobar replied as he broke open a window with his rifle barrel. "Zombie hole... Only..."

"Only what?" Jim asked between gun blasts.

"Only it was filled with food."

"What?" I yelled as I fired, pumped the shotgun-slide, and fired again. "Food?"

"Later," Jim said. "Out the window. The roof of the garage. Go." He protected the doorway, firing down the hallway. Escobar went to the window and peered out. Jill pulled the blankets off the bed and thrust it through the opening, offering protection from broken glass. Wilcox swung a leg out the window and swept the roof with his carbine before climbing through. Lopez pushed me towards our escape route as Jim shoved the door closed. The two of them slid a dresser in front of the door, but it wouldn't hold for long.

We went out of the window and climbed onto the roof of the garage. It was a steep-pitched roof, and the slightest slip would send one tumbling to the ground a dozen feet below.

Escobar jumped from the garage and landed on the roof of the car parked in the driveway. His bulk dented the roof, but he called for us to follow him.

Jill went next, landing hard and staggering off the car, her pinned and healing legs hurting again.

"Jump, Raz," Wilcox said as we shot zombies circling around the house on the ground below.

My fear of heights returned, and I froze. My eyes caught, uncomprehendingly, on zombies climbing up out of a bulkhead doorway to the basement of the house. That was how they got in. No one had checked the basement, but Escobar said something about food stored there.

"Jump," Lopez yelled in my ear and blocking out my fear of heights I leapt forward and landed on the car roof.

Climbing down into Jill's arms, I quivered in fear, propped up on weak knees and wondering how I made the leap. Jill's laughter at all the wrong moments brought me back to reality - it was a character trait that amused me.

Wilcox jumped and yelled in pain when he landed. Twisting sideways, he staggered and fell from the roof of the car, crashing to the concrete driveway.

I raised my shotgun in time to take the head off a zombie that closed in on us as Jill and Escobar helped Wilcox stand back up. Two quick thumps on the car told me that Jim and Lopez rejoined us.

"Let's go. Move out," Jim ordered.

"My ankle," Wilcox said.

"Can you stand on it?"

"No."

"You're going to have to." Jim moved to Wilcox's side, and with Escobar's help, they helped him run as fast as they could manage.

Excerpt from *Sullyland, A Las Vegas Mystery*

"Wake up, dead man."

"What?" I awoke to the muzzle of a gun staring me in the face. I focused and saw a large man pointing my gun at me. I contemplated taking the weapon, my handgun, away from him. I wondered if he had racked a round into the chamber.

"Get up. Someone wants to talk to you."

"Who?" I asked as I sat up and put my feet on the floor. The man was tall and wearing a black Canali suit. His Bertuli shoes backed away, giving me room.

"The guy you been harassing. Let's go."

"Oh."

"You think you're a big man taking a knife away from a kid?' The man backed to the doorframe.

I needed him in close if I was going to act. He seemed to suspect that, and he gave space with every step I took.

"At least I didn't kill him."

"He's my brother."

"You want to return the favor?"

"And not kill you?"

"If you insist."

"Ha. Get in the car. Today I don't get to kill you. Maybe later."

"Comforting to know."

The man smiled and backed down the left hallway towards the living room. Another man, shorter, fatter, ex-wrestler or rugby player, stood in the doorframe of the bathroom to my right. The man gestured with his gun and said, "Move it." He had a thick Italian accent. My guess was Tuscany, but I could be wrong. He swore slacks from a department store and a golf shirt. Black sneakers completed the classy ensemble.

We went out to the car; a white limousine sitting in my driveway. A driver and another man waited. The man had a shit-eating grin on his face as he hefted a double barrel shotgun. I could tell he loved every minute of this. Well, the day wasn't over yet.

"Where we going, Tony?" I figured someone might be a 'Tony.'

"Get in," the driver said.

I climbed in the back and sat facing forward, watching where we were going. Tall-Tony waved a gun inside and said, "Over there." Pointing to the backward-facing-seat. I complied. Tall-Tony and Stocky-Tony got in and kept their weapons aimed at me.

I rapped on the glass behind me. The window slid down. "No bumps, okay? We don't want any accidental discharges back here." The butt of a shotgun knocked the back of my head.

"Wise-ass," Tall-Tony said.

"Dead wise-ass," laughed Stocky-Tony.

I rubbed the knot that swelled up on my head. The window slid up. The doors closed. The windows were tinted dark, almost black. The men pulled shades down over the side and rear windows. I'd have to find Guiseppi's hideout on Google-Maps later.

"So what would Mr. Medici like to talk to me about?"

"What makes you think we are going to see him?"

"Because... When Mrs. Medici hired me, she didn't need four gunmen and a limousine ride."

"Veronika is nice, eh?"

"Mrs. Medici? She's a looker."

"She's very nice? Very pretty? I'd like to fuck her. He'd like to fuck her. Would you'd like to fuck her?"

"She's very pretty." I smiled. I tried too, anyway.

Tall Tony raised his gun. "You don't laugh. You don't talk like that. Only we get to talk like that." The two Tonys laughed. I frowned.

"Good. You frown. That's good." They laughed some more.

The remainder of the ride went about the same; with them telling stupid jokes and me keeping my mouth shut.

We got on a highway, probably I-15 but could be 215. We cruised at high speed for twenty minutes and then got off an interchange and went to highway speeds again for another five, followed by surface streets and six or eight turns. We stopped and the doors opened under a Mediterranean style shade attached to a Mediterranean style house. Good. We could be at almost any home in Las Vegas, or Los Angeles if the ride were longer. I looked around for the mountains. I could find my position in Vegas by the ever-present Sunrise Mountain, Black Mountain, Mount Potosi, or Mount Charleston.

A gun barrel in my back told me to move on. The men escorted me over the steps where another business-suited guard held the front door open. We all entered a marble tiled foyer and stood to wait. The guards put their guns away. We stood for fifteen minutes. The guards didn't seem to mind. I took a chair. It was one of those red cushioned and gold-gilt chairs similar to what you see in museums - the ones that have a plush barrier across them. The guards looked at me sitting down and at each other and shrugged.

John Medici came down the stairs. He wore a polo shirt and dress shorts. Sandals with white socks completed the ensemble.

"The sitting room." He said as he walked through the foyer. He didn't even look at me as he passed by, like one ignored a turd on the sidewalk. The guards motioned for me to follow.

We walked to the back of the house where glass windows opened up on a green lawn, sporting a large water fountain. To the right was a swimming pool where children played and dived into the water. Living in the desert is great.

We entered the sitting room where overstuffed leather couches circled a glass coffee table. A gas fire flickered in a marble fireplace. Two wildcat statues were chained to the hearth. One lay down, and the other sat up. Nice. Veronika Sokolov-Medici, wearing a bikini bathing suit and a flowery wrap sat at the end of one of the couches. Her bleach-blond hair was tousled. She leaned on her right hand, cupping her face. I could see tears in her eyes as she stared at the floor.

"Sit down." He ordered as if I was a dog.

"I'd rather stand. Giuseppe."

John motioned to his guards. I turned to them, clenching my fists.

"Okay. Stand." John stood also, and the guards spread out around the room. Tall-Tony took my Glock from his waistband and placed it on the coffee table. It sat eight feet from me. I might edge closer to it if the opportunity presented itself. I waited for John to speak his mind and would listen. It's important to do that with people who could have you buried in the desert.

"Giuseppe?" John's eyes opened at me.

"John, Giuseppe, Guido. Whatever."

"You are a tool. Aren't you?"

I shrugged.

"You were hired by my wife to follow me. To take photographs of these… supposed affairs. She thinks I'm cheating on her. She hires you so that she can divorce me. Take my children from me. Take my house. Take my restaurants."

"You are cheating on her."

John crossed the room in an instant and slapped me across the face. I could have easily blocked the blow, but the guards all took a step forward, and I watched their hands go to the grips of holstered revolvers and semi-autos. I held my pride for the moment. John stepped back and rubbed his hand. It must have hurt him; probably more than the slap did. I didn't rub my face. I wouldn't give him the satisfaction.

www.ingramcontent.com/pod-product-compliance
Lightning Source LLC
Chambersburg PA
CBHW021153130626
46554CB00005B/1792